A FATHER'S WORDS

A FATHER'S WORDS

A Novel

RICHARD STERN

ARBOR HOUSE NEW YORK

Manufactured in the United States of America

Designed by Richard Oriolo

Library of Congress Cataloging in Publication Data

Stern, Richard G., 1928-
A father's words.

I. Title.
PS3569.T39F3   1986   813'.54   85-26754
ISBN 0-87795-791-6

For my dear friends,
Imre and Maria Horner

A FATHER'S WORDS

1

I was raised by decent hypo-
crites to respect truth. My mother, a specialist in appearance, had the temperament but not the brains to be a
realist. For her, realism meant the essential crookedness of
things. Like many people who avoid introspection, she took
a hard slant on the world, looked for crooks everywhere, and
of course found plenty. Politicians, the executives of companies which sent her dividends—she never forgot losing
money in the McKesson & Robbins scam—the husbands of
her friends, were her quarry. Another was my son Jack.

About me, she was relatively uncritical. (Though once,
blaming a gas attack on my birth, she said, "I've had your
number from Day One.") As hard-eyed as she, I don't
ascribe this charity to maternal love; I think she was aware

that if I were a crook, the world would guess where I learned my stuff.

For more than thirty years, since I started a science newsletter, I've watched some of the world's best minds use the most refined techniques to understand the tiniest facts. It makes me skeptical about understanding anything complicated. Knowing isn't understanding. I've known Jack and my daughter Jenny more than thirty years, my other children, Ben and Livy, more then twenty-five. I've watched what's called their character form. I can track their decisions and actions to ones made decades ago. Is that understanding? No. I resented being fixed by my parents on the coordinates of my childhood. That is an occupational deformity of parenthood. Psychoanalysis helps with filial misconceptions; there's no science to free us of parental ones.

My father let my mother do his analytic dirty work. For him, she was priest and scripture. Ten years her senior and, by a wide margin, as our caste system went, her social inferior, his credo—I heard it for fifty years—was "Mother knows the score." "Listen to mother, son. She knows what's right. She does what's right." A butcher, and the son of a butcher, he'd exhausted his reality quota—my theory—heaving and cleaving carcasses. Good health, mother's inheritance, and earned fatigue relaxed him into roles he thought God-given: the Optimist, the Progressive, the Good Man, the Good Father. I grew within his indulgence and praise. Only occasionally, stuffed to the gills with his hallelujahs, did I point to certain imperfections in the world. His rebuttals were personal: he'd lived fifty—or sixty, or eighty—years, had *he* ever been raped, or murdered, or sent to a concentration camp? No. Had I? Had mother, God forbid? "Sure, Hitlers exist. So do bugs. Squirt them. They disappear. Who remembers Genghis Kahn?" Only in the last months of his ninety-two years did a few grim messages pierce his optimism.

Despite his myopic and mother's charitable—or shrewd—blindness to my faults, I've not been shortchanged when it comes to indictment. For my children, it's the household sport. Accusation, analysis, critical gossip, filled our rooms. "The Riemer Sound and Light Show" is my companion Emma's term for it. If I tell her Ben has criticized an editorial in the *News-Letter* or Livy suggested I donate my suit to Catholic Salvage, she isn't amused. When I told her that my longtime tennis partner, Seldon Dochel, said that I looked like a tightwad's purse, and that my granny must have let a Slavic missile into her silo, she wanted me to stop playing with him. I tell her Seldon amuses me. "It doesn't hurt me," I say. "And it's a cheap way of giving him pleasure."

"It's assault, Cy. It's undignified of you to allow it."

Emma looks tranquil as a pond, but ruffles easily. Talk of family particularly agitates her, but she has such a beautiful voice, clear, expressive, yet not the least histrionic, that no matter what it says, its message is that everything's just fine, the world's a beautiful place, just lie back and listen to the music.

I've always thought I was a loved father, as I am—on the whole—a loving one: semicompanion, semiprotector, and in the sense of lightning rods and orchestras, a semiconductor of my children's lives. At least the lives they lead when they're back—what they all still call Chicago—home. When they're here, it's hard to disentangle myself from fathering them in the old way. I feel I must be ready to take care of them, take them out to dinner and movies, tell them about books and truths. I like to know where they're going and where they've been.

They used to come home for Christmas. The reunions were full of nostalgia, stock taking, subdued competition, generosity, treats, and parties. The house—their mother's apartment—filled with old friends. I loved this, though in the old days I used to cast fiscal shadows over it: "I spend six months a year saving and the other six months paying off these Christmases." "Every snowflake costs me a buck." "This family's church is Marshall Field's." "Christmas, Verg won't bark unless he gets steak."

"Why conceal your generosity under pettiness, Dad?" says Livy. She is the youngest, smallest, and most intrepid Riemer. She interferes in street quarrels—"Break it up, you guys"—carries petitions through dangerous streets, takes risky jobs. She was a parole officer downstate in what Illinoisians call Little Egypt. Solid and cheery, her criticism seems part of something external, a performance, or an assignment: "Be aggressive now." Like many younger children, she's uncertain of her worth. Boldness has been her way of dealing with that. At her most forward, I can see a small fear in her lovely, clear eyes. It keeps me from taking her criticism to heart. She's a genuine improver, wants other people's lives to be better, knows mine could be a lot better. "If you only understood yourself."

Self-knowledge is her line. It's her problem as well. She doesn't understand her own gifts, her charm, her decency. As for me, she overrates my knowledge and underrates my selfishness. What others consider a virtue, she dismisses. "Why are you so anxious to know about things?" she asks. "You're going to run across the street to gawk at some historical marker and be hit by a truck. What's the difference where a treaty was signed? Or where some poet laid his

14

cousin? You know more about Darwin and Rilke than you do about yourself." Riemers are athletes of the mouth. Gab is our sport. We'll say anything to make a rhetorical point. (Witness this triple version of saying we talk a lot.)

"Sometimes you act as if you don't know who *you* are. You're interested in everything but Cyrus Riemer." I'm as self-centered as any man alive, but I can't tell her. (It would be seen as a dodge.) When she starts on me, I concentrate on her creamy face with its beautiful, whiskey-crystal eyes and lump of reset nose bone. (One of her clients broke it.) "You're the only person I ever met who won't skip a room in a museum. What's porcelain to you, Daddy? What does Mycenaean dreck actually do for you?"

"Who can tell where the clues are, Liv?"

"Baloney," but her face colors, she knows she's going a little far. "It's like a peeper claiming he's an anthropologist. He's a peeper. Period. But *you*. I don't know what you are. Maybe the cat that curiosity kills."

"It's a disease, Liv. What's the cure?"

She kisses me on the cheek. (Her own is warm with battle.)

"Doesn't matter. You belong in a museum yourself."

That's the cure: Dad as harmless freak.

A few years ago, Jenny, the oldest child, didn't come to Chicago for Christmas; the first time in her then twenty-nine years. She had the best sort of excuse—"excuse" is the way I think she thought of it—she was in Africa with her husband, Oliver, who's with the U.S. Information Agency. I felt the absence as the beginning of the end. (The end of family life.) Jenny, though the quietest child, is the bellwether. She looks like a Degas ballerina concentrating on a loose slipper in a cloud of pout. Like her siblings, she's fairer and rosier than I, but not so pale or red-cheeked as her mother. Agnes's appearance genes dominated mine, but our children don't look like her either. (Maybe nature decided our two lines had had it, except as elements of better compounds.) The children do look like each other, oval-faced, small-chinned.

That Christmas I said, "Jenny's cut the silver cord."

"One of us had to do it," said Livy.

"Why?" I asked. "Time and the world break enough as it is. We should hold on to what we have."

Even after Agnes divorced me, I felt this way. And felt that the children regarded our family as a happy one. "Tolstoy's wrong about happy families," I told myself. "They're not alike. Ours survived divorce."

I told Livy, "I guess the family is no longer the museum piece of your childhood. Still it's a good one." I was tempted to open up to her about myself. I didn't. She really wanted everything to be as it was.

Hypocrisy's essential in a happy family. So I keep transmitting my parents' credo (which, when I was growing up, infuriated me): Accomplishment, Decency, Cleanliness, Reasonable Honesty, Doing Your Duty, and Dirty-Linen-Should-Be-Washed-in-Private.

Because we have authors in the family, our dirty linen worried me. Ostensibly, our authors don't write about our family. I write about science. Agnes used to write about unhappy anteaters and ambitious hedgehogs. Jenny and Ben do write about families, but in a grand—literary and scientific—way, not a gossipy, revealing, and personal one. Still, their books disturb me.

Jenny's is a doctoral dissertation, entitled *The Wobbling Nucleus: The Family in Literature from Medea to Finnegans Wake*. Judging from Medea, I feared the worst. *Medea* is not about your average happy family. I'd always thought Jenny a gentle person, somewhat remote, a stray from a softer part of the universe, a Cordelia of loyalty. Why such a thesis then? "Oh," she said, "it has to do with rocking the family boat. It's the rocking that saves it." (Of course no one rocked the boat more than Cordelia.)

Ben's book is something else: "The first fetal history of mankind." Its title is *The Need to Hurt.* His notion is that the human condition is determined in the womb. Things have been decided long before the Oedipus complex. Ben shows pictures of a half-inch fetus writhing in a smoker's womb. "There is hell," he says. "The fetus, not the child, is man's father." He says all world leaders should be given fetal IQ's. "Why should the world have to reenact their placental troubles?" (What went on in Agnes's womb as she was having him?)

A family, even one as well behaved as ours, is an emotional hot spot. Its members have to be instantly alert to each other's feelings. This may be especially important in a well-behaved family, where character is formed, not only as a defense against one's own violent needs, but against rivalrous siblings. (Isn't Livy's aggressiveness the shell of the youngest child's need to perpetuate her cushioned infancy? And isn't Jenny's softness the crust which holds down the oldest child's rage at displacement?)

I asked Agnes what she thought about these antifamily books our children wrote.

She said, "You should be complimented your children study families."

Agnes is the great Smoother Over. (After twenty years, I was past smoothing.) The children made fun of her, but, in trouble, came to her, not me. She turned their jokes about her into compliments. "What's your opinion, Mom? Never mind. Shallow waters should keep still." This she turned into "I'm a person of deeds, not words." I got angry at them for joking about her. "Your mother doesn't need to gab. You children are her tongues. Who needs any more noise?"

However, my discontent with Agnes was clear to them. I was a tolerator—sometimes even a seeker—of boredom, but I found Agnes boring beyond toleration. I called her—the children heard it—"Mrs. Tedium Vitae."

We'd married right after graduating from Knox College. Agnes's father, Pop Lozzicki, a Chicago fireman with newspaper connections, got me a job at the City News Bureau, and Agnes got the first of her jobs in the public library. She also wrote reviews of children's books for *Library News* at three dollars a crack. Then she wrote and drew some herself. The third one, *Austin, the Anteater Who Hated His Nose*, was accepted by E. P. Dutton. One of the great moments of our marriage. With the fifteen-hundred-dollar advance—*Austin* never earned it back—I started the *News-Letter*. The office was our bedroom. (Passion lost a few rounds to print.)

I never tuned into Agnes's feelings. (I don't think she did either.) Under her dogged do-goodism, she had a dark view of things. It had something to do with those fire-disaster stories she grew up hearing. Pessimism became her vaccine. (It even got into her children's stories. Austin hated his nose so much that even after he found out how much he could do with it, it didn't lift him out of the dumps. That's why he never earned back Dutton's advance.)

Ease changes to unease so subtly. It's like the transposition of single letters changing a word into its opposite: *good* to *gold* to *geld* to *held* to *hell*. Not until Kraypoole, Agnes's lawyer—what a revolutionary notion that was!—summoned me to his leathery cave on La Salle Street and read me the caricature of myself he'd drawn from Agnes's discontent, did I come within miles of thinking of divorce. Of course, I knew marriage could be more than ours was, but I was busy and content. I hung by my teeth from the *News-Letter*'s weekly deadlines. That took all my energy.

Maybe Agnes's mouth should have given me the clue. (It's her equivalent of Austin's nose.) It's a loose, two-tiered mouth, like two mouths poorly joined, a mouth of contradiction, a skeptical mouth, a crook's mouth, though God knows Agnes is no crook. What she is, though, is unsurprised. Burleigh Fulmer, my Knox roommate, called her "Miss 'I Know.' " Saying little, she managed to suggest she was learning nothing from what you said. Her phrases are "of course," "naturally," "you might've known." From the horse's mouth to the crook's was a direct line.

Still, she was admirable, decent, good-looking. She hadn't altered much in twenty years. She was lean, she'd always been lean, the tendons were more exposed, the skin a little drier, the gray eyes more remote. I looked at her again, my old companion. We'd gone through plenty. Thinking about it excited me. In every way.

So there were oddly embarrassed touches, even more embarrassed withdrawals, embarrassed requests and embarrassing refusals. We were always polite, almost always silent.

I drifted off. Got out of the house. "Dad's going out again." Lectures, meetings. The Nuclear X. The Biological Y. The Science Writer's Z. X and Z wore skirts.

Agnes worked out the divorce. Or we both did, over the kitchen table, with pencils and papers. Hearts pounding, but keeping the lids on. A minimum of hassle. Lots of yielding.

"You take this."

"No, it's yours. You liked it."

Tears within every other word, yet easy and equitable as the cutting of ten million threads can be.

Jack was the child who took the divorce hardest. Or said

he did. If Livy's the Riemer who lets out most steam, Jack's the one who lets you know how much he's steaming. He's the family's self-dramatist, the family thermometer, the child who registers what's right and wrong with our lives.

I remember my first sight of him, ten minutes after he came out of Agnes, the brilliant eyes and the tiny red face held up to the glass of the nursery in the Lying-In Hospital. I remember the feel of Jack's head on my arm as I gave him the bottle, the mighty suck at the brown nipple. His first word was *ashes*. (More like *sshs,* from "Ashes, ashes, all fall down.") I remember his first step, in the kitchen, pounding the floor with one leg, then the other, staggering into Agnes's arms. I remember him, age six months, in the hospital after an intussusception—to prevent the intestine from "eating" itself—tied to the crib slats, so he couldn't scratch his stomach, tubes taped to his wrists and up his nose, my helplessness at his helplessness, the almost uncontainable love for that tiny person in the tiny blue hospital gown. He trembled in my arms as I carried him to nursery school. I remember pictures he painted—some of them are saved, one is framed—storms of color, as beautiful as Pollock's. I remember tense smiles as he looked at baby Ben: I was surprised and troubled by this excited tension.

Then the first flashes of deviousness. Lies, fantasies, evasion, inventiveness, hard to distinguish at the beginning. Perhaps this is always the case, but I remember it only in Jack. Words were more like things to him than they were for the other children. "For mama, with passion" he wrote, age seven. "Thank you, dear, but *love* will do." "I just love the word *passion,*" he said, "and I never get a chance to use it." I have somewhere a school paper on black magic with paragraphs in Latin copied from a book whose English he couldn't follow. When he and his pal Adam Sorgmund went at it, I'd put down my pencil and eavesdrop. With their great crops of hair, they looked like miniature Founding Fathers. Adam told Jack that his father—little Mel, the economist—was heavyweight champion of the world. "He licked Liston." Jack said that was nothing, his father—me—was president. "He is not, Ike is president." "Only during the day," said Jack. "My dad's president at night."

Invention slid into something else. "Benny saw an angel, Mommie," became "Benny took it, Mommie, not me," when it *was* me. Was Jack aware that his revisions weren't imaginative triumphs?

And on which side of the Nietzschean fence does he belong? Is he the "free man who knows himself free" and is, therefore, "competent to promise"? He'd say yes, but I—and God knows how many others—see in him only broken promises. He says he makes promises only to shut people up, he is fulfilling something higher. The rest of us are so far gone, we don't recognize it.

I think of a light bulb joke: How many Jewish sons does it take to screw in a bulb? One, if you don't mind reading in the dark.

If I'm unfair to Jack, it's because I know I'm both his model and his despair; he's the dye which shows up my inadequacy. Every fault I think I've overcome—or hidden—shows up in Jack; in spades. Deliberate caricature? Maybe. But what a waste of life, an existence based on exposing what your father's concealed.

This is abstract. Take something concrete, if easy. Clothes. I'm not much of a dresser, but Jack! For years he made a cult of sloppiness. When he first lived in New York after college, he bragged to me that he was the worst dressed person his age in the city.

Pathetic. Like some Anglo-Indian calling card: "S. L. Ramanujan. Candidate B. Oxon. Failed." The point is that my insouciance—or carelessness—became a cultish self-advertisement for Jack. He's what Nietzsche called "a masquerader in ascetic pomp." For years he boasted about how little he needed. Raw carrots and peanut butter sustained him. Yet he was a fanatic calculator of other people's dough and a practiced sponger.

Then too, he wanted to be rich and famous, to write great plays, court gorgeous women, knock the world dead. Till then, he made a cult of anonymity. He had no accounts, no charge cards, no listed address, no listed phone. Of his own, that is. His girls always had phones, apartments, jobs. And love for Jack. He evokes love. (Emma, who likes him, said, "Doesn't that mean that he has it to give?")

Emma has a strange sympathy for the children, even though she feels excluded from what she calls "the Riemersphere." She doesn't like them to criticize me or me them. Odd.

When I disagreed with Jack—about a movie, about his life—I felt his narrowness. (I thought it was stupidity.) "How could you like *E.T.?*" I'd say. "Or that damn picture with the jukebox spaceship? Your Spielberg has the soul of a Big Mac."

Jack said, "He's not *mine*. I know the pictures stink. I give myself up to them. I like being childish."

"My worry is you don't like being adult."

Silence and hard looks. I overreached myself. (Why should I punish Jack for the movie's puerility?)

"Come on, Jack, eat that fish. It's begging you to eat him."

"I'm not eating animals these days."

"It's a poor way to acquire virtue. What have the Jains accomplished?"

"Who're they?"

"They eat only fallen fruit. They accept the world as it is.

But cross one and I'm sure you'll hear a hell of a growl. I think I'll call you *'Desperdicio.'* "

"What's that?" I could hear a small weariness in him.

"Means 'scraps.' It's what they called the bullfighter Dominguez after his eye was gouged out in the ring, and he tossed it away."

"I don't get it. What does it have to do with me? Just cause I don't eat a lousy piece of fish?"

What *did* it have to do with him? I just felt like reciting this bit of lore I'd picked up in a book, yet I went after the connection as if everything had been thought out. "Not the lousy piece of fish. Your life. You keep tossing it away. As if it were a peel. You cover up by saying you don't need anything. One of these days, the world'll toss you out, and that you won't like." All sorts of color broke into his short-chinned face. He was holding back, being better than I. "Go on. What do you have to say?"

"You say everything. There's nothing left for me."

And he was up and gone, the napkin falling on the floor. I felt lousy. I wanted to call him. "I don't mean it, Jack." Or, "It's for you I say it, for your good." But what good? And then I worked myself up. Naturally—as his mother would say—*he* could leave the restaurant, *he* could make the big gesture. *I* had to pay the check. He paid no checks.

Unfair. He paid when he could. But when *could* he? Too few times. It was easier to walk out, to cut his ties, Fred Astaire, top hat, white tie, and tails, no ties and no connections, free for anything fancy. But Jack couldn't float like Fred.

Jack's character blunts what should be good looks. "I don't know why he can't look straight at you," I say to Emma. "Unless he thinks his character's being tested. Then he fixes you like the basilisk. And there's all that puffiness in his face. It's not right in a young fellow. You know there isn't a good picture of him after age five. His face just slips away from the lens. It's as if the light doesn't have any defined planes to settle on."

"Maybe it's you who can't settle on Jack." This is said sharply. (Emma doesn't like talking about looks, though she's perfectly lovely. Her father, a druggist, harped on them. Then, too, she was surrounded by cases of makeup and racks of magazines, which she got for nothing. No school in the world is more punitive than *Vogue, Glamour,* and *Mademoiselle.*) "You've got all those feelings—whatever they are—the reverse of the Oedipal ones. The Laius complex."

"Is that it? How can I tell? All I know is I can't tolerate the way he acts and looks. After all, he's mine. I helped shape him. His life's a rebuke to mine. And since I know his laziness and hypocrisy are mine, too, it makes it worse. The difference is *I* try to squeeze that stuff out of me. I don't think Jack tries."

"You don't know that."

"Sure I do. His way of countering things is confessing to them. He's glad to admit what a bum he is. He turns it into a boast. He's idle, vain, and boastful one minute, and the next decent, sweet, self-deprecating. 'Oh, I'm such a bum.' Yet I can't stay angry at him. The poor guy's got nothing."

"But your total attention. And Jenny's and Ben's and Livy's and his mother's." (Like me, she alternates defense and attack.) She says he reminds her of Prince Hal. "So when he reforms, he'll shine all the brighter."

"I hope that's his strategy."

"You know Jack's ambitious. Kind of crazily ambitious if you ask me."

"I know what he tells me, but he tells me such different

things. He thinks the world will just crack open for him one day, and he'll scoop up the pearls. One of those lucky sleepers whom the princess wakens with a kiss. That's why he loved that film about Stavisky." His favorite stories were about gamblers who risked and lost everything in one gorgeous burst; pretenders greater than their pretense; adventurers, swindlers, back-street Napoleons. These were Jack's heroes. Almost a hundred years ago, Napoleon opened the Pandora's box, and all over the world, Jacks— and Jills—dreamed of shortcuts to the moon. Was Jack like Julian Sorel? I wasn't convinced he was as smart as Julian or as high-minded, but where Jack's concerned, I don't know. There's much goodness in him, much sweetness. At least he pumps for the appearance of goodness. The way he tries to be the life of the party. He sounds like an anthology of good lines from *Sports Illustrated* and *The New Yorker*. Sometimes I'd call him on it: "I think I read that in Pauline Kael, Jack." He was—*no*, he *appeared*—unfazed. "I know her by heart. Isn't she wonderful?"

"She goes overboard a lot more now. Seeing all those movies drives you crazy."

"Yeah, I almost never agree with her now. But she writes beautifully."

"Most of the time."

"Yeah, now and then she really goes off the rails."

After I rock him back and forth like this, I hate myself. What was the point of it?

I tried direct suggestion. "It's often a good idea to work against opinions you hold. It frees your imagination. That's the way Rousseau started out, deliberately taking a contrary position."

"Tell me, Dad. I'm so badly educated."

"Oh, Jack," I'd say, but not aloud. The son who so offended could so easily melt me.

Yet under the sweet frankness, the authentic knowledge-hunger, the sad self-abnegation, there was also rage. Yet under *that* was—what? More sweetness? And under that?

Nothing about Jack was simple: corrected, faced-down, he acknowledged, he yielded, he apologized, he vowed, occasionally he even *intended* reform.

For years, I've called him late at night (after eleven, Chicago time, when the rates are low). In New York, where he usually lives, it's midnight. "I hope I haven't waked you."

"It's a relief to hear you, Dad. You blend in with good dreams."

This is telling me that I woke him up, but that his graciousness and affection are up to it. He's also dying to talk. The telephone has broken the dam, and out pours what he's seen and heard. Like a knight in a medieval romance, he touches stories out of every tree and fireplug. A waitress in his deli is the granddaughter of a Latin American dictator. The world's greatest quartet plays on the corner of Fifty-Sixth and Third. A billionaire's grandson bummed a quarter off him at the Pan Am Building. He turns Central Park into the Okefenokee swamp, a burger joint into Lutèce, street loungers, like himself, into wizards, sages, prophets, poets.

His favorite telephonic sport, though, is philosophic speculation. Was Schopenhauer right about the appeasement of the will? Is this the essence of Tolstoy and Gandhi? Does a healthy society require disobedience? Is Ruskin's welfare-of-one-is-welfare-of-all the answer? Is Camus right about capital punishment? Sorel about violence? Grotius about war? Is war essential to industrial capitalism, the only sufficiently rapid consumer of goods?

I interrupt his interrogative spiels with my own. "Isn't it more likely that war is the social expression of our souls? My God, look how we argued in the family."

"We didn't go to war." He's a great defender of the family. "We didn't shoot each other. Isn't that the point? A nation's a nation when it has weapons. Without them, you have bad feelings, not corpses."

"The planet needs corpses."

"That's what torments me, Dad. *Why?*"

Torment. I didn't believe that. "It's too expensive to settle on the phone, Jack. People like you have debated this since they measured time."

"Okay," he says cheerily. The cheer doesn't hide—and isn't supposed to hide?—disappointment. Disappointment at my dollar quantification of high-minded talk? Or is it just that the talk is ending for the night? Either way I'm in the wrong.

Our telephone sessions used to upset me so that I'd be unable to sleep. If Emma were at her own place, I might get dressed, drive over, and climb into bed. Naked, I'd lie beside her, happy in the familiar sleep heat and fragrance. Her nightgown might be twisted about her waist, her mouth babbling some sleepish esperanto. My body, touching the twin interrogations, would give the male salute. If it evoked nothing from the faraway dream country, I might study the familiar country, the little wheat field over the tender seam, the speechless mouth, the ribs, nipples, breasts, the gold hair asleep on the flesh, the secret odors from within, the respiration and rhythm of the body, which, engaged, could so change. Such old pleasure. The mind nailed by need, then the pulling of the nail.

If I was playing tennis in the morning, I'd set Emma's clock for six-thirty, then slide into sleep, watching the slow parade around its gold-ticked face. (At home, I kept no clock in the bedroom, because I needed the illusion of night's boundlessness to get to sleep.) If it wasn't a tennis morning, I got up early anyway and boiled water. I was not easy at Emma's place, nor she at mine. Her kitchen was cramped, and I don't like electric stoves. I burned myself there once and think the place is out to burn me again. I'd slam around looking for tea, find some decaffeinated phoniness, spill half the water, make a trail with the dripping bag from the stove to the paper bags Emma uses for trash. I'd sit by the window, which faces the white fire of the lake. The Outer Drive was thick with Loop-bound flies. At least, I wasn't part of that. I opened the window and leaned out to see if I could spot the parakeets. These tropic marvels appeared in Hyde Park a few years ago and stuck it out in their thatched rug of a nest through some of the worst winters in memory. Monk's parakeets. Green and gold with a pink cummerbund. With crazy luck they'd picked one of the few spots in Chicago where they'd be protected. (The mayor, Harold Washington, lived across the street; his bodyguards parked ten yards from the nest.)

When Emma gets up, she may or may not remember that I'd come. "Whatsa mattuh wiv my Fay?" She's wearing white socks, her curls are flattened, her eyes flecked with night confusion.

"Nothing. Couldn't sleep. Jack upset me again."

"Fay's leetle son knows how to ruffle him."

"My fault. I can't control my—whatever—for the way he lives."

Even talking baby talk—that pornography of lovers—Emma's voice was enchanting. It's like hearing one of those rare musicians—a Yo Yo Ma or Wynton Marsalis—who hits every note in the middle.

"He's like you. Won't commit himself."

"Don't use words like *commit*."

"That's what's involved here."

"You're too smart for that. Parallel lives, that's what ours are. Not entwined, like DNA. Replication is not what we're after. Anyway, we are *committed*—to many things, including each other."

"I want legitimacy."

"Another great word. Babies left in orange crates on Victorian doorsills. Dynastic wars. That's when you use *legitimacy*. Don't let other people run our lives."

"Who's talking? You drive over here in the middle of the night because your son says a few dumb things on the phone."

"People who want what everyone else wants are miserable."

"Easy for you to say. You've had everything everyone wants."

When I met Emma, she was cheery and hopeful. Because I was older, I drew her toward age. She had the cares of the aging without their experience, contentment, or resignation. Now she wanted the experience, marriage, living in the same place. More and more, she wanted this.

Recently, she'd decided her downs were caused by the pill. "I'm going off it."

We reviewed the options, including the snipping of my ducts. "I can't stand the idea of a knife down there."

"Okay. I won't let them cut my little Fay."

We settled on a spermicide foam. The nickel-size pill fizzed in the vaginal fluid. "From *caedere*, 'to kill,' " I said. "The fizz is the killer. If they pass the right-to-life law, we'll be indicted for murder." We didn't notice that one "contra-indication" was "occasional stinging pain." The pain I noticed, first as discomfort, then as a sting so barbed I spent hours lying in the dark, knees up, motionless, terrified I'd die of uremic poison. Emma is to ask her melancholy gynecologist, Dr. Wanny, for a better-tempered killer.

She says, "Ever read 'Hills Like White Elephants'?"

"No. Who—"

"Hemingway. A man wants his girl to have an abortion so they can live their great old life. She knows that means it's over."

"That's Hemingway. And the twenties. It has nothing to do with getting a contraceptive that doesn't scorch our privates."

"Maybe we should go with nothing for a while."

"Sweetie, you know my fathering's over. I've done my seminal job."

"I haven't."

Is she telling me something? There was a certain careless-ness the last pill-less weeks, a stupidity which, in the morning's bad temper, I saw generating another twenty years of raising Riemers. I'm not against new Riemers, am in fact mad for cuddling, cooing, and instructing them, but I'd passed on the generative job to Jen and Livy, Ben and even Jack. (Though I suspected he would always be his own child.)

"You know who I am," she says. "No beast is going to spring out of me because I have a ring on."

Yes, I know what she is. It's what I love, but also what I fear. Wonderful as Emma is, delightful, loyal, full of love, funnier than the funniest comics, intelligent in fifty ways, as pure in heart as people can be, there is also the Emma of self-hatred, hysteria, and despair. Self-hatred rotates with hatred of others, including me. Especially me. For as I am—she says—everything to her, I must be what she can hate as well as love.

When hatred governs us, I take to my own place where hatred reaches me only by phone. In a few hours, it burns itself out. What would happen if we were confined to one apartment?

Emma said we'd get a place large enough so that we could both be alone there. "Isn't that what your pal Rilke said marriage should be? Mutual defense of solitude?" I'd looked at three apartments with her and hated them all. I love my own place, the rickety wooden porch with the eaves where icicles hang, the blue ash which veils it from the other apartments in the courtyard, the exotic junk nailed and glued to the walls, old maps, prints, clay masks, a cowrie shell necklace, a Tibetan silk calendar, a West African fertility baton sent by Jenny, petrified limes and chestnuts, leaves and rotting flowers picked up as souvenirs from places, most of which I no longer *souvien*. I love the secondhand chairs, tables, and love seats which have learned to live with each other, the old Chicago brick and the gold which dawn and dusk draw from it. I love my dad's old chopping block with its blood groove and carrion smell deep in its fiber, the monographs, offprints, books, and old galleys piled like a paper San Gimignano on top of it. My being is expressed here.

Emma had her room here too. We called it the Little Room. She hated it. "You used to like it." "Never." God can't rewrite history. Anger can. So Emma didn't stay here often. I offered to swap rooms: "Fay likes Little Room." (A white cube with a maple bed, a night table, a wall of books, a captain's chair, a Korean scroll, an African market scene made out of butterfly wings, an upholstered piano bench with a pillow crocheted by my mother sixty years ago; her only artistic legacy.) The room faces northeast, the sun is strong there in the morning. Emma says the shade rolls up at its will, not hers. "And there's no space for anything but sleep." I say, "We'll knock down walls, make a big room. We could have it done while we're away."

"We're never away. And I'm tired of living at the Ibis. I'm tired of commuting." I understand this. I used to be the chief commuter. The routine—departure, travel, arrival, and then again, departure, travel, arrival—displaced everything else; the best moments were when I was safe in the car. "I don't want to die a TAS." One of our languages is acronymic. Makes the big small, the small big. Very American. HC is Human Contact (*seeing people*), DSU is Diet Seven-Up, HE is Hairy Eyeball (male lust), TP is Toilet Paper, LR Little Room. There is a large sexual lexicon. TAS is Tight-Ass Spinster.

"Never that, kiddo. You'll be the same. Being married is not going to make you big."

Big is a special word in our home game (where we reverse roles). She raises her arms in great-ape fashion and stalks me. "I've got you, my little Fay. I see your platinum hair, your ravishable little bod." (I am a two-hundred-pounder, Emma is blond and, though not small, slender and pixieish.) She uses a special voice, loud, orotund, snorty, cracker. "Come hyah, Fay, or Kong will mash yaw purty leetle haid in his hairy hand."

When Emma is down, I use another voice to pry her loose, a tough child's speaking through one of her pet animals, the orange plastic salamander, Feisty, or Blip, a two-inch pink-eyed hippopotamus. "Blip going punch Kong on hairy nose." From within her misery, Emma can hear that. (A therapist said that in depression she is five years old. "She can't be reasoned with, only played with.") Many times I thought, "I already have another child."

Now and then Jack got a job. That always cheered me. Even when the jobs were dreadful. The worse they were the cheerier Jack sounded about them. "What are you doing now, Jack?" I'd ask on the phone.

"I'm in a bucket shop. Selling cookbooks, diet books, save-your-guts, and save-your-soul books."

"Christ, it sounds miserable."

"I love it. It's the best job I ever had." He sat in a glass cubicle, walled by other cubicles. The air, he said, was "one black cloud of persuasion. When you make a sale, a bell goes off. And there's a supervisor listening to you on the phone."

"That's Orwellian," I said. "You quit that."

"Hell, no," he told me. "It's the best job I ever had."

I melted. Jack was no chicken. People his age were running African governments; in Silicon Valley he'd be called middle-aged. "Oh, Jack."

"People say fantastic things. I keep a notebook by the phone. They're sitting there with all this stuff in them. You call up and they explode. I'm here a month and I've got to buy another notebook. I'm trying to talk Jacqueline into quitting her firm and working here too. She's always complaining she doesn't have enough material."

"Who's Jacqueline? That's a new name to me."

"A friend, a writer. But she couldn't take the pressure here. I eat it up."

"How long can you stay at a place like that?"

"The average is three weeks. I'm already ahead. I'm tough. They can't embarrass me, they can't yell me down. I eat rejection. I eat screams. I don't give them a chance to say no. They say it, I don't hear it. Twelve calls an hour. We saturate a town. Edison, Montclair, Trenton, Mamaroneck, Rye, Yonkers, Red Bank. We're locusts. We take over the wires. We beat them down, block by block. We've got the ears of a whole town in our mouths. We chew down their resistance. They can't exist without us."

"You must be exhausted."

"Like running the marathon. When it's over, my head feels like the inside of a bell. There can be a million cars honking, and it seems quiet to me. We go off to a delicatessen—"

"Who's 'we'?"

"The other people there. Great people. Dancers, painters, actors, jugglers, future everythings. From everywhere. My best friend's an actor from El Paso. He's showcasing Trigorin this week. A great salesman, could sell you your own arm. He never lets them interrupt."

"Jack, wouldn't you be better off in a publishing house? You'd be a great reader. You've read a lot, you've got good taste. They couldn't get anyone better than you. And you'd have peace of mind."

"Dad, every humanities major on the East Coast is sleeping outside those places. I like the excitement of this. I need a little craziness. As for peace of mind, I've got all I want. Peanut butter, rye bread, and me. There isn't room for a bug, let alone a girl. This is all the peace I'll ever need."

Half of me reached for a checkbook—I wanted to get Jack out of there. The other half held back. Didn't everything that would count have to come from Jack's wanting it enough to move for it? The movement was what counted. Even mistakes would be swallowed by enough movement. (His, not mine.) "Are you on commission?"

"Almost. Eight more sales a day, and I get a bonus. Twelve more, and it's commission time. Real money."

Real money.

Older than twenty percent of American millionaires, for him anything more than five hundred dollars was *real money*. No Columbus has ever been such a mix of naivete and calculation. Yet maybe it was just as well to think your India was within reach. (Columbus's atlas had reduced the distance by thirty percent.)

A few years ago, home, for a vacation in his vacation, Jack asked me to take him to my bank to buy traveler's checks. He was off for another assault on Mount New York. In hand, he had a wad of filthy singles and a paper bag of change earned as a waiter (after I'd more or less forced him out of his room at Agnes's). "Hope you have enough checks," he said—not joking—to the teller. He had eight hundred dollars.

On the phone, I say, "I wish you weren't so lonely, Jack."

"I'm not lonely." He sounds ebullient, but the machinery of ebullience is audible. (And within it, despair.) "I've got all the company I need."

"Good. How about music? Do you get WQXR, at least?"

"No radio. I read. There's a paperback exchange around the corner. Fifty cents apiece. If it's a six hundred pager, I'll fork over seventy-five. I figure enlightenment by ten-cent increments."

"Sounds good to me. What are you learning?"

"That too, but I'm in it for—I don't know what I'm in it for. Life. Flowers. Honey. Jack the bee. And son-of-a-bee. Maccabee."

I can't bear his word playing. "Are you on something?"

"You mean am I high? Yeah. Talking to you is always a high."

And there was enough truth here so I almost groaned with pity. Was he so needy that even my probes filled his life? "Wish *I* could get high that way."

"Try books. I'll send you a package." For years he's *sent me things;* nothing ever arrived. *"Humphrey Clinker. The Crack-*

Up. The Transit of Venus. Analysis of Mind. Patriotic Gore. Great stuff. Have you read them?"

"Not one. I get straight F."

"Poetry too. You used to read it to us, remember? I never read it by myself till now. *The Ring and the Book.* I couldn't stop. I read it jogging, I take it to the grocery store, knocking down the Cheerio boxes."

"En route to the peanut butter?"

"Right. Yeats too. Really great."

"I've heard tell."

" 'Some burn damp faggots, others may consume/The entire combustible world in one small room.' That's my life. And it saves my life."

"I can see that, Jack. I used to write poems myself. Well, who knows, maybe you're on the right track. What the hell."

"It's not too late, Dad."

The conversation was turning upside down. Why not? I didn't have to spend my life laying out his. " 'A fifty-year-old smiling, public man.' Isn't that Yeats too? I'm not public and I'm not smiling, but I understand what he's getting at: half your energy going into facade."

"You've still got plenty inside, Dad. It's nice to talk without all this muck between us."

"What muck?"

"Oh, I don't know. You know. It's the wrong word."

"Words are all we have to go on. On the telephone anyway."

"Forget it."

I'd gotten to him. And what was the point of that?

Around my bed was the debris of the day's news, double sheets of the *Trib,* some windowed where I'd clipped items for comment in the *Letter:* wars burning up the world's body, in Africa's horn and backside (the Polisarios), its belly

(Chad), Atlantic flank (Angola), and inflamed South African toe; the endless ache in Europe's Irish ear; the gonorrhea in its Mediterranean groin. (That trouble was older than my namesake, the Persian Cyrus, dead in a desert war twenty-five hundred years ago.) Why fight my son?

He reported from a nearer front. "I went over to grand-pa's yesterday, first time in weeks."

Since he amused my decaying father, my mother tolerated him. "I hope you looked decent." Jack's baseball cap, T-shirts, ripped sneakers, and jeans upset my mother even more than his enthusiasm and fantasizing.

"Decent enough."

"What's up there? The old guy peeing in closets again?"

"No, but he was writing something I looked at."

"What was it? His will? Don't hold your breath."

"I'm not expecting a nickel from anyone."

"Good. Well, what was he writing?" I could see my father squeezed over the paper with one of the fat pens left over from the promotion of Riemer's Fine Meats. In black script on the white cylinders were the words for "Thank you" in twenty languages. With years of use, my father had learned and used them all. You'd bring him a glass of water, and he'd say *"Spassibo,* darling," or *"Salamat* a lot."

"It was crazy, all about rape, murder, abortion."

"I don't believe it."

"I didn't either. I was even scared to ask grandma."

"I hope you didn't."

"Sure I did. She knew all about it. It's his soap opera."

"What's that mean?"

"He writes down what happens on the soap opera so he can remember it next day."

"Oh, God," I said. "What lies before us, Jack?"

"You've got years and years to go, Dad."

"Can't tell, something can happen overnight." We'd just

published a piece that applied Thom's Catastrophe Theory to neural degeneration. Lots of Riemers had lost their marbles; it was a family distinction and could happen in a blink.

"At least Gramp can still amuse himself with TV disasters."

"Poor old fellow."

"He breaks my heart."

"It'll recover," I said.

"Well, good night, Dad."

Oh, Jack, I'm sorry." But he'd hung up. What the hell. He should know how his life embittered me. Look at him and then at my father, who'd put in thousands of honorable hours heaving and cleaving. All those loin chops and briskets of beef. He was proud as hell of his shop, his customers: Ted Lewis in the twenties, Joey Penner in the thirties, Balaban of Paramount, Nemerov of Russeks, Governor Lehman's mother. During the war, he was king; he dispensed chops like knighthoods. People offered him unbelievable bribes, he could have made a fortune. Not George Riemer. "No red points, no meat. Sacred obligation, Mrs. Klutznik."

From butcher to bucket shop in three generations. *La famille Riemer. Buddenbrooks. Rougon-Macquart. The Golovlyovs.* But an American father, even a skeptic like me, wanted some kind of log-cabin-to-White House in the family saga. What was the point of all those hours reading Jack *The Iliad,* explaining Darwin and Newton, Thoreau and Plato, the movement of blood and stars, of taking him around to Wright and Sullivan buildings, if, a few years later, instead of ruling the roost, he was nailed into one the size of a coffin?

Three weeks after that talk, we talked again. He'd moved into Jacqueline's apartment and made long but not collect phone calls to me, his mother, and God knows who else. He sounded gaga with happiness. I'd say, "This is costing you a fortune. Let me call you."

"Next time, Dad. Jacqueline doesn't mind. She's with Cravath and Swain."

"I thought she was a writer."

"She's gotta pay the rent."

"And you don't?"

"She's got a law degree."

"I don't care what she's got. I wish you'd pay your share."

"I do. Or at least I will. When I get another job. I couldn't take it anymore down there. What was the point?"

"You can't feel too great living off her."

"She gets plenty from me. Your Rilke lived off princesses and countesses."

"Jesus," I thought, but didn't say. "I think his publisher advanced him money. He'd published things when he was twenty. Anyway, are you a genius?"

"Never can tell. I'm giving it a try. Anyway, why should I live like people I despise? Jacqueline agrees. She's not worried. Why should you be?"

"Because I raised you, and it feels lousy to me. Like an empire with all those pukka sahibs living on other people's backs. Don't make your girl your wog."

Six weeks later, it was the same story. "Are you working Jack?"

"I'm writing an essay."

"Fine. On what?"

"Truth. Illusion. True illusions. Illusory truths."

"You should know a lot about them."

"I know what you're saying, but I'm trying as hard as I can. It's what I want to do. I'm not asking you for anything. Jacqueline and I are happy. She understands."

What the hell. I couldn't shame or infuriate him into—

what?—propriety? But I felt furious. Why? Was it resentment that Jack survived on nothing? Or was it proper revulsion at parasitism flying under the banner of other people's genius? "All these thoughts come into my head, Jack: a bloodsucker pretending to give a transfusion; gigolo-genius, with his Phi Beta Cock. Jack, the real geniuses are down there sweating with the rest of us, Einstein in the Patent Office—and it was no sinecure—eight hard hours a day, and he was blissful that he had another eight hours to work on his equations. Are you sure you couldn't bag groceries a few hours a day? Just for self-respect."

"Mine or yours? Look, I don't like having to ask Jackie for five bucks to have a beer. I don't buy clothes, watches, anything. A movie now and then, that's it. It's not permanent. A once-in-a-lifetime shot. If I don't succeed, that's it."

"I understand." Though my understanding differed from his. "I hope it goes well."

I even sent him fifty dollars. There might as well be a slice of Riemer charity in his cake. Though later, even this gift nipped at me: shouldn't Jack make it completely on his own?

A month later he called from Chicago. "I'm at Mom's."

"Is something wrong?"

"Not a thing. I'm in great shape. Just decided to move out of New York. I was never all that nuts about Jacqueline."

"You mean she threw you out."

"You know, 'Do this, do that, why don't you try this firm, go to this school, try that agency?' Nagging. I misjudged her." And she him, but she still "lent" him the air fare to get to Chicago. "I'm going to stay a week or so to see you and Mom. Then I'll head out. Maybe Houston or

Phoenix. What did you call them? 'Deserts of the soul?' 'Air-conditioned Congos?' " I'd written an editorial on the Sun Belt. " 'The Belt can't hold up the national pants.' " Jack knew how to please.

The week or ten days became a month, then two months. He exhausted his mother's enormous powers of endurance. I could tell from her voice calling him to the phone: "It's your father, Jack." Something in it said I was the only thing *outside* her apartment that Jack had. Yet Agnes would say nothing to him.

I did. "Please try and tell the truth more, Jack. You have so many little lies to live down. You've used up your quota. I say this not just as your father, but your double. *Ton semblable, ton frère-père.*"

"What's that, Dad? I can't catch French."

"Your double. Your fraternal father."

"I appreciate that. But I only lie when it won't hurt anyone."

"Very noble, Jack. But the world doesn't let you get away with that."

"What's the world know? All the saints were losers there."

"Christ in heaven." Had there been something in the explanations of Plato or the circulation of the blood that had spun Jack out of orbit? Or could it also be congenital? Whatever, that such a combination of openness and concealment existed not in the pages of Dostoevski but in my own son was an agony for me.

Jack often said that I knew him better than anyone else. "Yet he doesn't really know me," he wrote Jenny (who told me.) "He knows me through my faults. It's as if he's sealed off that part of me and preserves it. He only had three digits of my number. Yet that he can love me, knowing these, knowing how much crap I'm full of, gets me."

Ben, who, as a boy, had admired him most, now felt he was a fraud. "I can't stand his falsity, his con, his laziness, his boasts of a higher calling. He acts as if only he knows how to live."

"Ah, Ben," I'd say, "Jack doesn't have anything."

"Who's to blame for that?"

"Right, but that makes it worse for him. He's really a good boy."

"Boy?"

"In a way. He's much more a boy than you. He knows he's wasted years. Our job's to help him. So he can have some kind of decent life."

"I want him to have a decent life. But I can't stand his bullshit. The only way he can get attention is to be a creep and a phony."

"That's not the whole story. You know that."

"I certainly did know. That's what hurts so. The way I was taken in. It shouldn't affect me, but it does. I can't help it. The way I feel I don't want to help it. I just want to say, 'The hell with him.' "

Feature by feature, Ben looks like Jack (gray eyes set back in short-chinned oval heads too small for their features, especially the imposing schnozzolas), yet, though they are clearly brothers, they look less and less alike. Ben is gaunt and gangly, yet he's handsome where Jack everywhere misses handsomeness. In Jack's face, childhood and age collide. He's losing his hair and his pink skin is picking up lines. He hates getting old and deals with it by simple subtraction. "If I want to call myself twenty-six or whatever, who does it hurt? It's nobody's business but mine." Hearing this, Ben said, "In a couple of years, I'll be your older brother."

"You're ahead of me in every way but years, Benny."

"Please don't say that," said Ben.

You never could tell when Jack would do something un-Jack-like. (Was that the point?) When he first lived with Sondra Bieber, he got a job with a consulting firm and within a month discovered a flaw in their traffic procedures that saved them a hundred thousand dollars. He did research on condominium conversions and published an article about it in *New York*. I was thrilled. When I told him I was, he said, "It's not serious work. Any fool can do it. Any moron can make money."

"Maybe so, but why not continue to make a little then? A few bucks in the bank won't kill you. Other things can, though, and you don't have any health insurance. It's been seven years since I had to take you off my policy."

"I can go to the clinic."

"Sure. For splinters. But wait'll it comes to something serious. You think your mother and I'll let hatchet men work on you? You'll bankrupt both of us. And your sisters and brother too."

"I didn't think of that. It's something I'll really have to consider."

"If you get the forms, I'll pay the premiums till you get settled in something."

"I wouldn't think of that, Dad. Thank you, though. I'll do it myself."

But didn't. The world wasn't going to break his legs or infect his lungs. It was still his oyster. Insurance was for wimps.

Phones.

They always got Jack in trouble. The latest installment

comes in a letter from Sondra. (I had no idea he'd gone back to her.)

Dr. Riemer, when the phone bill arrived yesterday, I nearly had a heart attack. $942.00. Nine hundred and forty-two dollars!!! I mean, what was Jack doing? You'd think he was a corporation lawyer. But I know what he is. I guess you do too. When we lived together, he was always on the phone, but there was nothing like this. I'm not going to take it, I'm calling a lawyer. Here I let him live rent free, because he said he was on his own and had no place to go to. I'd thought he was married. But you know Jack. When I said something, he just looked through me. I've never met anybody who could wipe out problems like Jack. Anyway, I was in the country for eight weeks and I let him stay. So there he was like on a foundation grant. Except I'm not a foundation. I'm only a girl who used to feed and fuck him, and who made the mistake of letting him use my place. Nine hundred forty-two bucks. Can you explain it, Dr. Riemer?

Oh, Sondra, if I *were* a doctor, if I had the wisdom of a thousand doctors, I couldn't come close to explaining Jack. He's had trouble with phones for years. At least phone companies had trouble with him. It was one of the first signs he wasn't kosher. His telephonic fooling around started when people were discovering chinks in the tele-phonic dike. *Esquire* published a piece on virtuosos of long distance who'd learned to mimic the tones that tie the ends of the earth together. They had nothing to say, no one to say their nothing to, but spent hours filling the world's wires with their fraudulence. This is what Jack and a college pal did. Ma Bell—another lost love—traced it to the college— poor Oberlin—the college traced it to Jack, and I got a letter which was a forerunner of Sondra's. (Jack has always been easy to trace.)

Sondra, I told her in my head. *I do think your generation took to the phone as mine did to the car, as twelve-year-olds today take to computers. The phone annihilated confinement for you, offered you that convenient combination of intimacy and safety. I understand this deeply myself. What Quasimodo was to Nôtre Dame, Jack is to the telephone. He inhabited it, haunted it, raided from it.* Wacht am Phone, *Sondra. The bill you cite is staggering. Nine hundred dollars is a sum I cannot associate with a private telephone bill. Yearly, let alone monthly. And I have had to call contributors all over the country. Could there have been wild parties there? Centering around the telephone? When I was twelve, I called people in the Manhattan directory to tell them they'd won Horace Heidt's Pot of Gold. Once, there was such excitement at the other end, remorse ousted devilry, and I called no more. Perhaps there is a phonic gene askew in us Riemers, Sondra. You can blame me here. Anyway, your letter, understandably overwrought, leaves me puzzled. I shall get hold of Jack and get the story from him. Then I will arrange to see that you are compensated somehow or other.*

What was Jack doing at Sondra's anyway? Had he and Maria—his wife of six months—split? Even if I was the last to know, I should know that. I telephoned him and got the sepulchral voice—is it a humanoid projection of electric current?—which said, "That number is disconnected."

Disconnected.

Jack's true note. I had a daymare of seeing him hurtling like Satan into the void.

There was more to Sondra's letter:

Should I tell you what this place looked like? The filth, the vodka bottles and cigarette butts, the bathtub? Did he store coal there? I haven't done an inventory but as of now I can't find books, tapes, cassette decks, And, Dr. Riemer, I can hardly write this, but there are smears on my wall—silk paper at seventy dollars a yard—that

look—and I haven't the nerve to smell them—like shit!!
Your son, sir. What kind of pariah did you raise? Have
you published articles in the *News-Letter* about such
behavior? Maybe you could explain it to me then.

What can I write her? *Dear Sondra. I'm agitated enough to
ask if you have the right Jack.* I know she does. *Riemers do not
smear excrement on walls. That is not our style. Jack is basi-
cally—though I know what a difficult concept this is—a good
person, a modest and self-doubting person. Surely you know this too
or would not have taken him in. For which he's surely grateful. As
am I. Despite the mysteriousness of the circumstances, the appalling
conditions of your apartment, despite his momentary disappearance,
he will come through for you. For both of us. For himself. As for
the phone bill, what can I say? Another mystery. A woman out
your way just received a phone bill of a hundred thousand dollars.
It was delivered in a truck. All a mistake. Some finaglers had
bilked her. If Jack's your finagler, you will be reimbursed.*
Every line of her letter twisted in me. Despite my new
doctorate—from the University of Sondra's Anger—I felt
like a pariah too. *Pariah.* I looked it up. From the Tamil for
"drummer." Jack *is* a noisemaker, beating his own drum. (To
compensate for hollowness? No: using his hollowness as an
instrument.)

No, Sondra, I've published nothing in the News-Letter *which
explains him.*

11

The spring before my mother's death, Jack was back in Chicago again, hanging around Agnes's place, watching ballgames, reading, wearing Agnes to the bone. When she came in the door from work, *he* went to work, yacking away with all the goodies he'd stored up.

She called to tell me. "I think we should do something for Jack."

"What's up?"

"Well he is. He's got all this energy. Naturally. I come home from work, all I want's a bath and a drink, but he's charged up. He's very sweet, but he overwhelms me. He tells me everything in the paper, everything he's thought. And he wants me to respond."

"I'll speak to him."

She put him on the phone, and I suggested he take it easy on his mother.

"I'm such a dummy," he said. "I'll hold off till dinner time. I've got all this on my mind and no one to tell it to, all this energy—"

"Maybe you could channel it into a job."

"That's not a bad idea. Let me kick it around a little."

The next day I made sure I lost the first and third set to Seldon. Walking to the car, I said, "You were too much for me today."

"It's my new forehand. I hold my thumb on the groove, so my power works for me. But you were sharp too. You had me in the second set."

"I lost concentration in the third. I'm worried about Jack."

"Jack? Oh, Jack. Your kid. What's the matter?"

"He's been back here a month, moping around Agnes's."

"Agnes? Oh, yes, the ex."

"He's wearing her down. He's got all this energy, and it's got nowhere to go but his mouth. I've dropped the suggestion he might devote an hour or two to making a little dough."

"A Riemer thinking of dough? How vulgar."

"Just enough to pay for his grub. I think he wants to, but I also think he's scared of being turned down. He's no chicken, you know, he's twenty-nine. Seldon, I thought there might be something for him down at the Exchange, or in your office."

"No problem, Cy. There's always something. But do you really want him working down there? If I didn't have a nut the size of the Hancock, I'd quit tomorrow."

"I think Jack would love the noise and craziness. He loves gambling, and despite protestations—you sometimes think you're talking to Saint Francis—he loves money. I think he'd function pretty well down there."

"I'll find something for him. Moshur always needs someone. He goes through gofers like farts through silk. He'd be good training for Jack; in case he's ever on death row."

To my surprise—for despite what I'd told Seldon, I wasn't confident of budging Jack—an hour after I told him Seldon had said to come down, he was on his way to La Salle Street, and two days later, he called to say he was working for Moshur.

"Terrific, Jack. I'm delighted for you."

"And I for you, Dad."

After a month on La Salle Street, Jack had the confidence of a company raider. Intoxicated by the fortunes swelling and breaking around him on the Commodity Exchange, he flowed with financial wisdom. "You should get *your* money working for you," he told me.

"My six-thousand-dollar nest egg? Show me how. No, don't. They're about to double the cost of third-class mail. Do you know what that's going to do to me?" The *News-Letter* relied entirely on subscriptions. "I may have to fold this tent."

"I'll see if Felix can think of something."

Felix Moshur—Jack's new hero—was my age but acted, according to his new devotee, like the Western world's prime stud. His clothes, cars, body, apartment, and girls were all terrific. His hero was Jacques Brel, the manic, melancholy Belgian singer. There were Brel tapes in Moshur's cars and houses. He sang along with them, sobs and all, while he drove his two Porsches or his Alfa Romeo. He was tanned and barbered by artists. "You should see his shoes," said Jack. "I've eaten worse steaks. The seams are *stroked* on. And what blazers. Nino Cerutti with real gold buttons." He knew where Moshur bought his ties, his belt buckles, his suits, his girls. "He's not like your pal, Dochel, the Panter. If harelips were in style, Dochel'd have an operation. It's two totally different countries at the office. Dochel's a schnook. At the end of the day, there isn't a bump of confidence left in him. Moshur just floats, and the deals follow him. I know, I add up the trades every day. Tuesday, he made four million."

"What did he lose Monday?"

"Sure, he can drop two million. He does it like you buy a chiclet. Money's nothing to him. He gives it away left and right. Yesterday, he gave Jules, the winter wheat man, a car."

Moshur also passed on his girls. "On the whole, as it were," said Jack, "I'd prefer a car. Some of the girls are okay, but most are poodles. I see them down here waiting for him. They're just service stations for him. He gets fueled up, uses the john, washes his face, and says ta-ta."

"You should write a brochure, Jack."

"It's great to watch him. He really moves. You know, you look at most people in the world, they just sit around waiting for something to happen."

"You've got my number."

"No, Dad. You've got a soul in motion. But most people just sit around and wait. Moshur moves. So fast he's always *there*. Like some vase people can't wait to put their flowers in. He opens his mouth, the grapes race to crush themselves on his palate."

"Oh, my Jack." Extravagant, yes, but it had been quite a while since anyone had drawn so much out of him. I closed the censor's office and said something about Moshur being quite a fellow. With Jack necktied, jacketed, shaved and shorn, it was clear something good was happening.

He started coming up to see me about once a week, sitting on the cushioned pew I'd picked up from a dismantled Baptist church and drinking the Dubonnet he brought with him. (It was a Moshur drink.) A huge postage hike had gone through and was followed by a forty percent boost in printing costs. I was very low. "I don't know how long I can hang on. I can understand Evich." He'd printed the *News-Letter* from day one. "He's losing customers left and right. Because he hasn't switched to cold type, he has to lean on those who stick with him. The price of loyalty. But it couldn't come at a worst time. It's the madness of those damn free-marketeers. Racketeers in Wall Street drag. They want the Post Office to break even. They don't ask the Defense Department to break even. Some priorities. They don't know general welfare from General Electric. The country was born in print, its future lies in people knowing what's going on, so what do they do but nail us poor publishers. The truth is they don't want people to know what's going on. They're like muggers, they work best in the dark." On and on. It was my topic these days, everyone around me was tired of it.

Jack followed along though. "History's just smut to bureaucrats," he said.

"That's too easy. I know plenty of enlightened people down there."

"You knew them in Chicago. You don't know them in Washington. In Washington they turn into their desks. 'A soldier shouldn't be fired by his own gun.' You see it on the Floor too. Brokers standing around, no movement, then, all of a sudden, someone makes a move, and in five seconds, the place is a riot. No reason. Mob contagion."

Low or not, agree or not, I did love talking with Jack like this: two men swapping views, no meanness, or, anyway, not much. He looked well, too, his face less puffy, his eyes steadier, instead of ducking away or trying to outstare mine. He hadn't been so much of a piece since boyhood.

"I mentioned your problem to Felix, Dad."

"What problem?"

"You know, the *Letter*. Postage, printing, the whole business."

"What's the point of that? It's not his business."

"He's a smart guy. He thinks the answer's advertisements."

"Where would I advertise? *Time?* That would be my revenue for six months."

"No. Advertisements in the *Letter*. People advertising there."

"Is he nuts? Who in the hell would advertise in the *Letter?*"

"Felix says the big thing now is Personals."

"What's that got to do with me? I have a selected and a tiny readership. If they have lawnmowers—or for that matter, computers—for sale, they're not going to advertise in the *Letter*."

"You don't get me. The big thing now is that every person is ready to acknowledge that he's got needs. Your readers are human too."

"I see." I sometimes looked at the *New York Review of Books*. "You think we should provide for the sexual comfort of our readers."

"Is it so horrible? 'After your hard day with the silicon chips, spend an hour with an understanding person, Ph.D. in biochemistry. Write Wilhelmina van Blumberg, Box 2H.' "

"What would we do if we got an answer?"

"We send it to Wilhelmina. There are plenty of Wilhelminas in laboratories. They have exactly the same organs everybody else has."

"Very neat."

"Felix thinks you'll not only have ad revenue, you'll double your subscriptions."

"Which'll double my postage."

Nonetheless, to my surprise, I let the idea work in me. I'd been softened by resentment at what threatened my honorable little enterprise; and by curiosity. Besides, Jack said he'd handle everything. In a moment of what-the-hellism, I said we'd try it for an issue. We actually had a few ads already—aerospace technicians *wanted* or *wanting*—they were fillers at the bottom of columns. I myself had used them a dozen times to ask for information, books, articles, or charts. Anyway, in the next issue of the *Letter*, down at the bottom of an inside page, went Jack's teaser—not about Wilhelmina van Blumberg but Dr. J.L.C., Box 32A.

Did this demure insertion do the trick? Or did Jack underline the ad and get it posted on university and industrial bulletin boards? I don't know, but to my amazement, there were twelve apparently genuine responses to Dr. J.L.C., and in the next ten days eight personal ads were sent in, all along the lines of "Biophysicist, Bloomington, seeks scientific and personal exchange with young woman in the field."

"They'll learn how to do it," said Jack.

By the third issue, we had a quarter page of ads, not just Personals, but ones offering software, cars, and summer rentals. It meant two hundred dollars an issue. Even more surprising, there were seventy-eight new subscribers. The extra money didn't entirely compensate me for the embarrassment—though I never talked about the ads and nobody but Jack, Seldon, and Mel Sorgmund mentioned them to me. I did get used to their presence, and to the money.

I read them all myself. Though Jack said he'd do it—and did—I didn't completely trust him. I had to police my own grounds. He took care of the "postal arrangements," the "boxes"—which were a corner of the pew—and the initial exchange between responders and advertisers.

One day an ad came in which threw me. It went something like "Wanted: partner in truth. Truth = id, id = force, force = hatred, hatred = excretion. Exchange shit for jism." When Jack came up the next day, I said, "This is the end of the line. We're drawing madmen. We'll have murderers next."

"This is a fluke. Or a joke."

"Either way, we've stirred up muck."

"Send it back. But I think you're overreacting. You and I are word people. Words don't mean the same to most people. The guy's probably been sitting on this idea for years, maybe tried to turn it into a piece for the *Letter*. Finally he just couldn't hold it in. He's probably not up to making a dirty phone call."

"I'm no child, Jack. I carry as much garbage around as the next guy. But I'm an editor. I'm responsible for words. Even to them. Here's a fellow who reads the *Letter*, which means he's got to be reasonably informed, reasonably intelligent, even reasonably responsible. One day he reads these ads of ours and they make him think he can just take off, and that we'll print it. It wasn't just a passing thought, either. He had to type it out, address the envelope, put a stamp on it, and throw it in a mailbox. All social movements. My job is to do something about it."

"Sounds rational, but I still think you're overreacting." He must have seen in my face that this was the wrong note. "All right, Dad, *that's* not my business. I just want you to consider that you're thinking of throwing the baby out with the bath. More and more ads are coming in. You can raise your rates, keep the same space. And you decide exactly what you print. You don't like, you don't print. Or you rewrite."

A week later, the following arrived.

In 1968, the Supreme Court said you could watch whatever you want in your own home. We know what you want; we have it. People want to see celebrities taking it up the a—— and down the throat. Wonder what President R—— R—— and Prime Minister M——— T—— do when they get together? We'll show you. Want to see the "beautiful people" looking great and acting greater? We've got the films!!! Write for our catalogues. They include numbers of accommodating pals in your own area. (Not Alaska, Hawaii or the Dakotas.)

In a rage, I called Jack at the office. "What the hell! How did lowlife like this even hear about us? You've really got me in a hole now. I'm just not going on."

"Dad, this is my fault. I'll explain, if you calm down. The guy is someone I know. Or someone I know knows. He just misunderstood what he could say. Notice it says, 'Proposed Copy.' He's willing to let any version go in. Twenty words advertising his films and that's that. He's willing to pay triple rates. And he'll run it for six issues."

"You know about it? I can't believe it. Jack, that's betrayal. Parricide. I'm ashamed of you. I know you think I lead a rodent's life, but it's my life, and it stands for something. It's not up to you to—do me in."

"That's too strong, Dad."

"It isn't. I agreed to these Personals. I was angry, and I was greedy. I've felt lousy about it. Even on the way to the bank, yes. But all I have, Jack, is this little enterprise, one that counts for a few hundred people. Suddenly, it's open season on it: just come on in, world, and shit on *Riemer's Letter.* I can't forgive myself. Or you."

"You will. I'll talk it all out with you. Later. It'll be all right."

That night, I said to Emma, "It's an attack on me. He found a way to punish me. Acting out his mother's anger."

"What are you acting out?"

"I'm a son too. I've been there. All this suppressed fury determining your life. Invisible, but there, like Arabic vowels. All those fights Agnes never had with me. Well here they are. Ben and Jenny's books. Even Livy, handcuffing all those tough guys. One way or another, everything comes out. And then it's Mount St. Riemer. Boom."

"What do you want from them, Cy? You don't want them melting in front of you, bringing in daddy's pipe and slippers for the rest of their lives. Jack's right. You're overreacting. That's what you should be looking at. Not at them. Anyway, what have the other kids got to do with the ads? They haven't even mentioned them to you." She'd washed her hair. It was wound around wire cylinders and pulled beyond the pale hairline. It lengthened her face and made it look strict and hard. "What's this, Emma? I didn't ask for good sense. I've come home to port. For comfort. Out of the storm."

"Some storm. You don't know storms."

"What's with you?"

"You know," she said. "You know."

I didn't, though sensed she was looking back of me, beyond the occasion. I was not just the father of my children, I was Angry Father, the old Aurora pharmacist who, among other injuries, had died too soon, before she'd finished college. Talk of protein chains, *this* is what humans passed on: fury. And there was more. She must have sensed a threat to her in my rant about the children. Jack had pulled the stopper on my anger, and she couldn't tell where it would stop. "You're scaring me, Cy," she said in what we called LV, the Little Voice, and she held out her right forefinger and pinkie in the Italian cuckold sign that was our shibboleth of peace.

The Robusto ad had come to Jack through his new girl friend, Maria, the filmmaker's daughter. They'd met at Moshur and Dochel's, though for the last few months, she'd worked for her father in the converted warehouse on South Ashland where he filmed and packaged his movies. She lived with her divorced mother in Park Forest and, until she changed it to Robusto, had kept her mother's reclaimed maiden name, Pengratz. ("It sounds like something Daddy uses in his films," she told Jack. "What a relief to unload it.")

Jack said most of the Robusto family worked in the warehouse, Grandpa and Grandma Robusto in the mailroom, various uncles and aunts handling sales and building sets. "Some sets," said Jack. "Polar bear rugs, chandeliers, wine racks with flexible bottles. They should pay Dali royalties. Maria thinks her father's just another tycoon. She says Singer's sewing machine let every woman dress like a duchess, Eastman's camera let anyone be a Michelangelo, Ford's car turned everyone with four hundred bucks into an Arthurian knight, so her pop's out to make every man a king where it counts most, in the sack."

Maria turned out to be a charmer, a tall girl with a lot of brown curls on a forehead that's a little too impressive and eyes that're a little too brilliant to let her pass for one of the girls who starred in her father's productions. She had a charming laugh and laughed a lot, though I thought her humorless. Smart though. Straight-A smart. And witty, but within all the charm and wit and musical laughing, I felt even then the kind of metal none of my own kids had, some fierce undisplaceable hardness. I enjoyed looking and listening to her.

She started coming up to my place with Jack. They sat together drinking Dubonnet on the velveted pew amidst the technical magazines, old *News-Letters* and galleys looped over the old butcher's block. Even though I'd rejected the ad—it hadn't disturbed her, she'd been trying to do her boyfriend's dad a favor—she kept making the Robusto pitch. She had nothing to gain, this is just what she did. She sat there high-browed and sparkling beside cheerily naive, poetically grasping Jack, with his shortchanged jaw, uncertain gray eyes, and the rosy cheeks out of the Polish-Scotch-Saxon genes which had outchemicaled mine. She had, she said, smelled out my "old-fashioned, Puritan fears. It's so wasteful, Mr. Riemer." She had a darling child's smile, self-consciously mischievous. The dimples in cheeks and chin were entrancing. "It's so simple. Why should people in need have to conceal it? Why shouldn't everybody be in each other's arms? You're so busy with all this," patting a stack of *Letters* as she would have a chihuahua. "You don't know how starved human beings are, how full of bad time they are. That's why they're sick and dangerous. Assassins—there are studies—spend nine-tenths of their time fantasizing and masturbating in front of the TV set. Daddy's films could do a lot for them. I know they're not much for you and me"—*that* she didn't know at all—"but at least they have a sort of reality, and then they can call the telephone numbers and there'll be real people on the other end. Maybe not your type or mine but real voices, real bodies. Instead of confusing what's inside and outside their head and blasting the confusion away with a gun, they can see real people and talk to real people. It's not so different from the knights with the Grail, or the saints with their God."

"You're a missionary, Maria."

Out came the dimples and a beautiful laugh from between the perfected teeth. "I know you're laughing at me." I shook my head. "I know the films are awful. Like the magazines and the parlors, but this is the biggest business in the world. I'm not going to stay in it, but I respect what Daddy does. He teaches all these scared, dumb people how to go about things. How not to be ashamed. How to meet people. How to get down to lovemaking."

And so on, a combination of Boy Scout handbook and science fiction. There were plans for international networks of sexual combination; erotic satellites; comfort stations in computers. The next stage would be chemical creativity—Beethoven in one pill, Newton in another—because except for fossil holdouts in the sticks, the sexual war was won. It was time to use Robusto money for something else. Her father was giving her a roving commission to start new enterprises. "The kind of people who write for your magazine are the kind I'm looking for, Mr. Riemer. I'm sure if you cared to, you could play a big part."

Afternoon light stroked stacks of offprints on geomorphology and sensory deprivation, complex tidings from the world's laboratories, and there was this full-jawed, dimpled Danton in designer denim chirping utopian baloney.

"Old codger Riemer," I told Emma, "listened as if it were a lecture on spindle-burst sleep. She practically made me a millionaire. Sitting right there in my computerless office Fossil Inc. The last man who still uses a typewriter, who can't play electronic chess, who still has to snuggle up with a book under his own light in his own chair."

"Quit being so proud of not being with it."

The talk about Maria's ambition upset Emma. She'd just had a bad interview at a data-processing firm; the personnel officer had told her she'd taken the wrong courses. Where was her Fortran? Her Basic?

"We're both fossils," she said. "Except you still fit in. The *macho*. I'm just *hembra*. Lady Zero."

"You fit better than I. Or Maria. You have more ideas just kidding around than they have all year at General Electric. The detoxification tank for ex-celebrities; the orbiting spaceship for ex-dictators; the phony clipping service for nonentities. Pure genius."

It had been a bad winter. Our cars seldom started, and Emma was marooned in the Little Room at my place more than she liked. Tears were frequent. She was between jobs, between courses. She felt she'd forgotten how to look for a job. "I don't even know how to make a resumé anymore. There's nothing I can put on it that stands for my life."

"Perfection of the life or of the resumé."

"Another week without a job, you'll feel about me the way you did about Jack, that I'm a bum and a parasite."

"That isn't the way I felt. And he's not a bit like you. You've supported yourself since you were sixteen. Don't worry. The winter's demoralizing. Wait till it warms up a bit. You'll find something right for you."

"Sure. The world's panting for me."

"It needs you more than it knows."

"There is no 'it.' Not even Robusto films would use me. The world's a series of nos. You don't know what it's like."

"I know. I'm lucky. I haven't looked for a job since I started the *Letter.*"

She slept poorly. She'd fall asleep at nine and wake at 1:00 A.M. Sometimes she called random numbers in later time zones. "May I speak to Dr. Arbuthnot?" Usually she'd tell the operator she'd dialed the wrong number, but if the voice on the other end was sympathetic, she talked for a while. A woman in Los Angeles spoke with her for twenty minutes about Balzac. My February phone bill was triple its usual size. "I'll pay you back, Cy. As soon as I get a job, I promise."

"It's on the house, sweetheart."

She went through catalogs—the bulk of her mail—filling out order blanks for a dollar ring here, a nail brush there. Our apartments were full of carved animals, hammered brass, beads, earrings, bracelets, a hammock, a wicker bird cage. "Want some Royal Oregon pears for your birthday?"

"No."

She ripped the catalog and arched it toward the wastebasket. She has a special catalog toss, a release of comic triumph, every disposal an accomplishment.

"Do you think I need FDS?"

"What's that?"

"Feminine deodorant spray. It gives you ICR."

"?"

"Instant Crotch Rot."

A great present giver, she began giving Christmas presents in October. When she finished a course— she'd taken enough for three degrees, if there were degrees in Eccentric Culture—she gave the professor a present. "Doesn't it look as if you're bribing him?"

"A little circle of fake stained glass? A dollar sixty-nine? Not much of a bribe."

"Your funds are getting awfully low."

"And you're terrified I'll be living off you. Well, I won't. I can always turn a trick."

"Keep on losing weight, you won't be strong enough to turn the key in the lock."

Pili Shastri, a friend from her Modern German Thought class, suggested she go to her doctor. Pili, a tiny woman with a handsome thick-lashed face, wore beautiful saris and a Brahmin caste mark. "Do you see how well I look, Emma? Two years ago I was puffy. Do you remember? There was sickness in every pore." She rolled up her sleeve. "You can see the health in my skin. The flesh is pure. I used to have migraines, my head was filled with lightning. Since I've gone to Dr. Smark, I have not had a touch of headache. An hour with her and hell dissolves from my life. She's a genius. Has degrees from every country in Europe. I want to make an appointment for you."

"What can I lose?" Emma asked me.

I started to say, "Money," but, after all, she needed something.

Not, however, Dr. Smark, who turned out to be a tiny old lady in a red wig who gave Emma bits of dried fruit and vegetable to hold in her palm to determine "what your nature requires." What Emma's nature turned out to require was bean extract, rutabaga, and Dr. Smark's own concoction, marmoset liver pills. "She said I've abused my system for years, told me I had eight pounds of 'fecal matter' in me. Not all bad news, though. It seems I have a 'highly evolved skull'—"

"I could have told you that."

"—and exceptionally good whorl patterns on my fingers. Said I reminded her of Greta Garbo, whom she cured of hemorrhoids with blueberries and Rye Krisp. She also took care of Charlie Chaplin's bowels. Or was it Beethoven's?"

It was the winter that Emma first thought of another cure: "Maybe we should have a kid, Cy."

The summer I think of as the one of Mother's death began with a party to which Emma and I didn't go. Maria's father, Italo Robusto, gave her a twenty-fifth birthday party. That was the family billing. The public billing was a Benefit for the Hopi Indians. Said Jack, "They'd better not get their Hopis too high. You can imagine who the real beneficiary will be. Mr. R., cleaning up the Robusto act. Isn't it great how much *schmutz* you can cover with a benefit." He was sitting on the windowsill facing me, the sun flashing from behind him into my eyes. "Maria and I aren't enthusiastic. She may not show up. She hates birthdays. Now hers is up on billboards."

"How so?"

"Poppa R.'s making a thing of this. He's inviting everyone in the Celebrity Register. Who knows, one or two may even come. He's trying to get the Field Museum for it. Probably wants to pump champagne out of the dinosaurs' mouths. Innocence and *chutzpah,* what a combination. He has no idea how much social clout you need to take over a place like that. Then he asked Maria to write Balanchine. He wants to commission a ballet."

"At least he's heard of Balanchine."

"He knows how to turn on the tube. He asked me to leak it to Kup and Aaron Gold that Balanchine's doing one. He assumes they won't check it out, so he'll win either way. Winning means being in the paper. Balanchine or not, it's going to be one great fiesta. Girls dressed in orange blossoms, period, then stripping them off one by one. The petals'll be tagged with numbers for prizes. Except every prize is priced. Tax deductible, for the Hopis."

"Ingenious. Maybe we should give a party for the *Letter.*"

"He's trying to tie in with Neiman-Marcus. Wants to give away yachts, helicopters, islands. Not just cases of Chateau Margaux, but the chateau itself. You listen to him, you know he can't be serious, he knows it, he knows you know it, but that's what excites him. He sits back a yard deep in leather cushions, a foot of Cuban cigar sticking out of his face, and this gold buttercup in his lapel he tells everyone is the Danish Legion of Honor. He got it for judging a Porn Film Festival. I heard him dictating an invitation to the Saudi royal family. I said, 'Mr. R., there're three thousand of them. You'll have to hire Soldiers Field.' He said, 'Maybe they won't all show.' If they do, he'll sell them Arizona and they can take the Hopis back home with them.''

"Well, it'll be some birthday party."

"If it's one percent of what he wants, it'll be awful. I want Maria to get out of it. But she's got a bug in her bonnet, and she's put it into his. It's the laundering of Robusto dough with all these grand social projects. And from there, who knows, Mars. She's already gone around to talk shows and colleges. Scattering change for good causes. Way down deep, as deep as I see anyway, she wants to be president. Wouldn't be the first hysteric in the office."

Was the worm already in the apple? Or was Jack's lyric tongue outrunning his feelings? "Do I smell trouble?"

"I don't know. The usual seesaw. One day, she's full of flash and gumption, everything clear, the world just a row of small hurdles she can take one at a time. The next day, she spends an hour choosing a lipstick, worries how to pronounce a word, is terrified of being seen with the wrong person, forgets to turn down the gas and goes crazy when the pot's scorched. Yesterday she threw a load of wash in the garbage can instead of the hamper and cried for half an hour. Take a look at this." He touched a pink lump on the rim of his left ear. "She gives me haircuts, I save a fortune. Until yesterday, she'd never touched me. It hurt, but you should have seen her after she saw the two drops of blood. Out of her skull. She wanted to lick 'em. I don't know if we're going to make it."

We didn't go to the party, but read about it. Jack said Robusto hoped *Women's Wear Daily* and *People* would do pieces about it. They didn't. Not that the party differed much from the ones they cover. It didn't take place in the museum but in the ballroom of a hotel—the Sherman—that was due for demolition. The girls weren't dressed in flowers and nobody stripped; the prizes weren't oil fields, islands, and yachts, but watches, TV sets, and Betamaxes. There was a hundred-pound birthday cake whose remnants were carted off the next day to the Little Brothers of the Poor. The Hopis were sent a check, though it was unclear what the amount was. The *Sun-Times* made it half a million dollars, the *Trib* fifteen hundred.

August was my vacation month. (There was no September issue of the *News-Letter.*) In palmier days, when there were science conferences, I could squeeze fare and some expense money out of the sponsors. That was before Vietnam dried up the money. The summer of Mother's death, money was especially tight. I couldn't afford the trip east, though Mother, I knew, was in rotten shape. (Back in March she'd tripped in the street and broken her arm on the sidewalk.) Anyway, I didn't feel like spending time with her and my father. I filled the vacation days with chores, cleaning out *News-Letter* junk—manuscripts, galleys, offprints—painted window trim, sanded and strained the dining room table. I read a lot, sometimes at the Oak Street beach, though I dislike lying around in the sun.

In Stuart Brent's Bookstore I flipped the pages of a book called *The Annotated History of Here,* an inventory of a nonentity's house, a list of the phone calls and mail he received in a week of his useless life.

Bui Doi, "the dust of life"—Vietnamese for the orphaned street children in Saigon—that's what I felt about this (and almost everything I saw in the streets, the beach, the mirror).

"I'm losing my grip," I told Emma.

"You're gripped by griplessness." She'd read Heidegger in Modern German Thought. "You're falling into falling."

"Write that up on your wall and I'll study it."

Emma wrote slogans in silver eyebrow pencil on a huge red heart she'd painted above her bed.

Actually it made sense to me. I wasn't getting anywhere. Partly, it was discouragement with the *News-Letter*. More dust.

Jack said, "Cheer up, Dad. The *Letter's* doing better than ever. More and more people are going to find out how useful it is. Has anyone complained?"

"Not in words. There've been no words. Except from Mel." Sorgmund wrote he was surprised and delighted at the ads. "You've been able to separate your mission from bottom-line necessity," he wrote.

I answered, "You confuse bottom line with derrière. Still, I appreciate your taking the time to write. I feel like the little girl Einstein helped with long division."

Sorgmund answered my answer. "You not only have new revenue, but the satisfaction of denouncing its source."

The ads.

I liked to think they were off in a corner, a place I sprayed for bugs and forgot about. The only people beside Jack, Maria, and Seldon who mentioned them to me were Mel and Erwin Evich, the printer. *That* was a surprise. It was the only time Evich had ever commented on anything in the *Letter*. I used to say that he recognized only letters, not words, but no, the old fellow with workman's skewed shoulders and iron eyes one day narrowed them into something like a leer and said if that lady chemist who played the oboe and liked trekking was all she said she was, he might answer the ad himself. "Though if trekkin's somethin' done in the sack, I won't be up to it."

Nothing sexual surprised me anymore. If the pope answered an ad from Queen Elizabeth, I wouldn't blink. But I was surprised at Erwin. "I never look at them, Mr. Evich."

"You'd get a tickle from it. It's good to see what people are doing. Most of your stories're about rats and bugs. People like to read about people, Mr. Riemer. I don't interfere with my clients' business, but a few pictures wouldn't hurt either."

Right as rain, Mr. E. But my readers had to get their print kicks elsewhere. As I did. Because I'd started checking out the ads myself. At first, it was amazement at the solemn cleverness of the advertisers: "Systems analyst seeks unsystematic diversion." Then I began handling them. Jack showed me the routine of checking them, estimating and dispatching the bills. For a while, I did it automatically, only occasionally noticing the text and then with amused superiority. Some of the answers came back to our "boxes," which were an alphabetized box of letters under the butcher block. My job was to remove the outer envelope and put the address of the advertiser on the sealed envelope inside. It took me twenty minutes to do the biggest pile. One day, addressing an envelope, I realized it contained a picture. (Sometimes the responses were so thick I had to add postage.) I turned it over, the flap was loose on one end. I got out the kitchen knife I use as a letter opener and worked it in and down the flap. No go. I was going to tear it. A telltale tear. That should have stopped me. It didn't. I went to the kitchen, boiled some water, held the envelope over the steam until it loosened. Inside was a letter and in the letter was a polaroid of a naked woman, short-haired, snubnosed, with strong breasts lifted by her pose. She stretched back on a lounge in the middle of a grassy lawn. The letter read:

> Dear L.Y.M.,
> You asked for a picture! Here's one taken last summer at my cabin in Beverly Shores. (Less than an hour from Chicago. Take the Interstate exit Gary East, then Rt 12.) I too know how silly all this is, yet it's human nature! You may ask who took this picture. It was a man I met the other time I answered an ad! (If you and I work out, I'll give you the gory details!) I did not ask you to send a picture, but I don't mind your asking me for one! My motto is Nothing to hide! Take it or leave it! I'll leave things in your hands now. You can write or telephone. I'll wait a week before thinking you found what you wanted elsewhere!!!
>
> > In hopes,
> > Stephanie!!!XO

A short-nosed, short-haired, well-built woman of thirty-five, maybe forty, with a cabin in Beverly Shores and an ex-lover. Solid legs, full breasts, face poorly focused by ex-lover, sunlight in the hair, which could be brown or blond. I checked elsewhere. No help. A hand covered her—still private—parts.

I looked at the picture for fifteen minutes: excited, amused at my excitement, then excited some more. And fearful—even here, alone. *Dear Stephanie. I found this letter on the street, couldn't resist opening it. You're gorgeous!!! I also like your prose!! Sorry about L.Y.M. I am C.R., the man who wants to put your breasts and everything!! in his mouth.* For relief, I went through other letters, feeling for pictures. There was one. More excitement. I steamed open the envelope and drew out a snapshot of a fat man pointing to his erection. Nonetheless, I became the steady voyeur of my advertisers and their pen pals. Part of my routine: Monday, laundry; Wednesday, bank business; Friday, peeping. In six months, I saw fifty or sixty women, half of them more or less naked. Many photos I wanted to keep—inside, say, the *Journal of Bio-kinetics*—but I could no more ask Model Camera to reproduce them than I could run in the Chicago Marathon. No, I restricted myself to the steam, the contemplation, the resealing, and the maintenance of an internal portrait gallery. Though almost no erotic time—alone or with Emma—was unaffected by it. Courtesy of Emma—or myself—I made love with thirty or forty new bodies. (Emma was surprised, pleased, and sometimes burdened by the revival.)

In one of my thousand small arm encounters with my mother I said, "You're not just a superficial, you're a superfluous person."

Half a foot and—as I saw it then— fifty IQ points, and five thousand books shorter than I, she came back with a response that undid these disadvantages: "Wouldn't that mean you were superfluous too?"

I'd seen her in action, nipping at cabbies and store clerks, putting on terrific airs—I think she was trying to vault miles clear of the terrible meat odors of her husband's trade—but there were spunk and hunger for life in her. She read every word of the paper, belonged to the Book-of-the-Month Club, read *Newsweek* and *Commentary*. She was regarded as an awesome intellect by her friends, the aging ladies with whom she played canasta and bridge for a twentieth of a cent a point. That day we'd been arguing, not about our usual disagreements—my sloppiness, my increasing weight, my failure to inform her about the minutiae of my life—but about politics. Her diminished physical powers augmented her pessimism and fury at the world and those who ran it. "Deadbeats, that's all they are. Every one. That sneak in the White House. That German liar who advises him. What an accent. Kike. You wouldn't see him at Quakerridge. That actor-governor in California. Can't pronounce his own name. Thieves, ignoramuses, bums." She'd been reading a life of George Washington. "There's a man. Never took a nickel. Wouldn't dream of using influence. Was afraid he had too much. Loved education. Felt he didn't have enough. Wanted people to get every point of view. No Plumbers then. No sneaks. No Huston plan."

"It's much harder to run the country now, Mother. Washington never had to please anyone, he never campaigned, never had to promise anyone anything to get a vote. Look at the guff modern politicians swallow to get anywhere. Kowtowing to these fast-mouth vacancies who splice the TV shows; kissing rears from Maine to Mexico. They have to be iron men."

Mother was fierce, her clear dark eyes—passed on via me to Jenny—were still fine and clear in the river-rich map of her face. "That's it. By the time they're in office, nothing's left. So they filch. I've seen it all my life. Since Franklin Roosevelt, there hasn't been a decent human being there."

"What about Ike? You loved Ike."

"Yes. Honest, a nice face. But a dummy. Look at his vice-president."

"Mother, what do we know about these people? They work like hell, all of them. We couldn't do their job in a million years."

"Who'd want to?" said Mother, shaking her thin old arms, the flesh waves aflap at the elbows. "We do our jobs, we mind our business. We're fair."

Jobs. Business. It was my hatred for what I saw as her lifelong idleness that undercut the authority she'd had when she was only my mother. I sat in her immaculate living room, the midmorning summer light making silver nodules of her beloved trinkets and doodads. What was superfluous? What was necessary? I looked that up. Out of *non cedere*, "not yielding." What was need? Out of Gothic *nauths* (from *nau*, "to press closely"), "compulsion."

Mother sat on a straight-backed chair whose cover she had crocheted when I was learning to walk. How much of me was she? Were my powers bounded by hers? What cartography was refined enough to clarify the ways we related to each other? Two piles of human stuff, one about to crumble, mouthing off on another summer's day in the long history of life. How do either of us matter to that? I wondered then and wonder now. Maybe the most that can be said is, We mattered a little to each other. And how did we show that? Not beautifully.

I said to Emma, "Sometimes I feel I'm nothing but my bonds." (Meaning, that's why I don't want anymore.) "Just a depot of connections."

What you saw was a small, busty woman with very bright black eyes and wavy brown hair (which I saw as brown years after it was gray). Strong-willed, a nagger, a boss, yet also more honorable than most, certainly more patient and dutiful. (Though she couldn't bear to wait on lines, wait to be served in a restaurant.) My father's mind had softened. (A degenerate hippocampus.) Fifty times an hour he asked her the same questions, "How old am I?" "How many children do we have?" "Who are you?" When she told him who she was, he wept. He sat in an armchair by the window overlooking Third Avenue. The *Times* was in front of him, read and reread all day long (always fresh, because always forgotten). Every few minutes, his hand went to his bald head and the tips of his fingers rubbed and scratched at the place where, nine decades ago, the hemispheres of his skull had come together. Was he trying to tear himself away from his flesh?

He inquired often about the time. Mother never said, "What does it matter to you?" She sensed that it did. There was the time to get up, to get dressed—he wore a coat and tie every day—there were his three mealtimes and teatime, there was the day's walk to Central Park.

She didn't think about his time being up: he was her occupation.

Ten years before his death, when his mind was still all right, I gave him a Woolworth notebook and suggested he write his autobiography.

"I couldn't do that. I haven't had the kind of life worth such a title."

"You've had a wonderful life and you're a wonderful fellow. Everybody's life is precious. Things that no one else has ever known will disappear from the world when you do. It doesn't have to be a great book. Anything you write, I'll love. So will the children. And it'll be good for you. You'll remember all kinds of things you can't remember now." The old fellow had beautiful blue-green eyes set deep under still-black eyebrows. His bald head showed the intensity of his decision. He was the sort of fellow who carried out everything he tried. (My young displeasure had been that he'd tried so little.) Somehow or other, he decided to do it.

"He takes notes all the time, Cyrus. Sometimes when he's dummy at bridge, you see him light up, out comes the notebook, he scribbles in that miserable butcher's hand of his. Laughs out loud. 'What's so funny?' I ask. 'You'll see.' He thinks he's Dickens."

He didn't. He was a modest man. The family baby, when his mother died, his four sisters pillowed him with love. He stayed innocent, optimistic, an ideologist of progress. Misery and crime made no impression on him. "There've always been murders, craziness. Things are far better now than they've ever been. Have *you* ever been murdered? Have I ever killed myself? New York is the greatest city on earth. It's the safest city. It has the best meat, the cleanest water, the most wonderful theater, the most beautiful parks." He'd scarcely been out of New York, never out of the country. I'd long since stopped contradicting his chauvinism.

Family.

Out of the Oscan *famel* meaning "serf." (I got this from Jenny's book and got also her notion that the family rose out of property and service.) Most of the literary families in Jenny's book are for the birds; monster makers: Medea's brood and Lear's, the Golovlyovs, the Rougons, the Mac-quarts, the Snopeses, the Pollits (in that grim farce *The Man Who Loved Children*). My charming Cordelia of a daughter suggested that the family might be obsolete. Family was as "useless as the eyes of cave fish, the hind limbs of the manatee." (Did she get this from a *News-Letter?*)

Surely the old institution still counts, if only in a different way from the ancestral model. Biologists use the term *labile:* so the "useless" mesonephric tubules turned into the ducts of male sex canals. America was born of broken families and has had very few oligarchical ones: Adamses, Astors, Roosevelts, Rockefellers, Kennedys. And in literature, where are our Buddenbrookses, our Thibauts, Bennetts, Forsythes, Rostovs, Shcherbatskys? Except for Faulkner's Compsons and his Snopes, our writers celebrate loners—Ishmaels, Dimmesdales, the Twain boys, the James girls, the Augies, Holdens, and Nathans diving off creaky family boards for the unknown. Family for us is the Mafia or July Fourth, when we're One Big Family. Though the Founders were not much as fathers. (Mother told me

Washington couldn't bear his barrenness, kept hinting to the end that Martha would produce another George.) As for Lincoln, he had no luck with wife and sons.

For me, family counted. Though I was not much of a son (and perhaps not much of a father), I've taken—foolish?—pride in family. My old shame of my butcher father and butcher grandfather is gone. I remember Grandpa Riemer with something like love. His red ties, red handkerchiefs, red nose, are bits of love in my memory. I remember his pride that he had "every plant allergy a shitty man can have," pollen, grass, fungus, even, it turned out, the sawdust from the floor of Riemer's Fine Meats. He spoke of the "conshpirashy"—he never mastered the "s"—of the vegetable world against him "becaush I wash a butcher." He told me stories of Budapesht and his "astonishment" in World War I when the United Shtates fought, not againsht the terrible Frenchmen but the Germansh. Till then, his dear daughter Susie—Shooshie—had scratched out the faces of French soldiers in the Rotogravure. Some of his books are still around my place or Agnes's—Maurois's *Disraeli, The House of Rothschild, Of Human Bondage.* A handsome, fastidious, and immaculate man away from his bloody trade, he was vain of his silver hair and mustache, the diamond stickpin in his red ties, the spats of his fine boots. His hatred of ugliness is in me. He stuck his red nose in and out of the room where mother and her pals played bridge. "Oof," he said. "The harpiesh." He took back moves in checkers before I—his five-year-old grandson—jumped his pieces. That's an endearment now, a possession.

I'm even prouder of my Schein connections. Though, of course, ashamed of the pride. When my cousin, Marcus Schein, invited me to the opening of his African art collection at the Metropolitan Museum I nearly split with it. That someone in my family should be part of the Great Museum of my boyhood intoxicated me. "It goes against reason. Against everything I believe," I told Emma. "But there it is. I'm thrilled. I'm tempted to go."

"Respect the logic of feeling," said Emma, instructing me with my own instruction.

In New York, I made the same pitch to Mother. "You know you want to go. When's the last time you got all dolled up?"

"When I looked more like a doll."

"Don't word-fence with me. Fix your face. Let Angelica work on your hair. Put on that black lace thing, your diamonds—my God, they'll name a new wing after you."

"And what'll I do with your father?" who sat there smiling at our occult persiflage, music to him, the lovely old exchange between the two loves of his life. I'd spent the first half hour fielding his questions: "Where do you live now, Cyrus? Ah, yes, Chicago. A beautiful city. We've been there, haven't we? Very beautiful. Not New York, but a great city. What's the name of that mayor? Ah, yes, Daley. Give us this day. No La Guardia, but quite a man, isn't he? How long have you lived there now, Cyrus? Long as that? My God, you must like it there. Do you have children? Wonderful. What are their names? Of course I know them. I love them all. It just escapes me what their names are. Tell me once more."

I responded casually, imitating as well as I could my mother's long patience. She and I sat at the card table playing Hollywood gin with fierce—concealed—competitiveness.

"Bring him along. He looks grand in a tux."

My father's blue-green eyes, bright and indifferent as a

roadside flower, glinted with something else. "What's that? Who'd look nice?" We'd not respected him, he'd sensed the treason.

"Cyrus was just saying how well you look in a tuxedo, George. He's going to wear one tonight, he's going to a party."

"And I'd like you to come too, Dad. You and mother." Betraying her, for I hated—as I shared—her shame. Hers went back to the butcher shop, the low meat-and-slaughter trade, which the Scheins, her family, disdained. I had shrunk from disdain, but then I was her son as well, safe in that. I hated the stupidity of shame, blamed it on her, and punished her with it when I could.

"No, we can't go. It's too hard to stand around in that chilly museum. I told Marcus and Aimée we couldn't go. Even if Dad were up to it, I'm not."

At the Metropolitan Museum, gussied up in my thirty-year-old tuxedo with its satin lapels, my belly imperiling the old seams, I handed the invitation in at the north entrance and went up the escalator in a crowd.

Marcus's collection filled four enormous rooms. Among the long dresses and tuxedos were bronze crocodiles looking greedily at wooden fish. There were fang-toothed masks of hysteria, straw gushing out of their heads, five-foot-long tusks carved into spear carriers and grain grinders, wild cubist heads stopping calabashes, antelope headdresses of cowrie shells and gold, a wooden bowl held in a rainbow-colored hand carved "by the great carver Olowe of Ise."

Scheins, Glucks, Becks, and Firetucks made a museum within a museum. A kissing museum. A hugging museum. "Cyrus," "Jean," "Cyrus, honey." "Aimée." Marcus's wife, long-nosed, fine-lipped, still beautiful: "Oh, Cyrus, I never thought you'd come. I couldn't be happier." There was George Gluck, who, forty years ago, had taken me to hear Schnabel play the *Waldstein* and *Hammerklavier* at Carnegie Hall; Lawrence Beck, mother's doctor. And there was Marcus, the great cartographer with his timid green eyes and great bald head, the eastern rival of Rand-McNally. He had taken me through his office when I was at Stuyvesant High School, showing off the gleaming tools, the fine frames, the cartouches and double-nibbed pens. He'd held a geologic map up to the window with two fingers explaining its glittering blue strata. "Beautiful, Cyrus, isn't it? To make the complex clear is a beautiful as well as a useful thing. To represent depth on a surface. Beautiful. What's depth anyway but a pile of surfaces? We are attracted by this surface or that, and when we think we have a depth of surface, we say we've fallen in love." The timid green eyes filled with randy glints. "We should say we've risen in love. Right, Cyrus? Our little non-Mercator projections. Ever see the anther of a tiger lily sticking up in the sunlight? Such pride in these little ups and downs. Do you know Turing's theorem, Cyrus? Though you're a literary boy, ain't you?" Back then I wrote poems, was one of the editors of the Stuyvesant literary magazine. Now I know Turing's theorem: every process with a finite number of stages can be automated. I think I remember thinking what a strange map Marcus's was, with its tea-colored eyes and Floridian schnoz. "I think it's possible God's a map," he said. "Not a mapmaker, a map. The Map which equals what It represents. The Map that loves Itself." I'd thought, what a nut.

All around us in the museum were fanged heads, wooden snakes, gorgeous spears, tuxedoed cousins. I put my arms around a shrunken Marcus. "Do you remember your wonderful lecture on maps to me?"

"I remember it perfectly, Cyrus. We had beautiful days together. I give myself credit that you've gone into science as you have. Am I wrong?"

"No, you're not wrong." Who knew, maybe he wasn't. Though it shouldn't be a boast for him. "I wish I could do you more credit, Marcus. If I'd had your gifts, perhaps I'd have won a Nobel Prize, instead of telling people what prize winners do."

Downstairs, away from the caged African nightmares, amidst potted shrubbery and trees, a trio played "This Can't Be Love Because I Feel So Well." I did feel well, here among my great-beaked cousins, hugging, kissing, congratulating, dancing, generation with generation. There was lots of triumph here, triumph of possession, arrival, display. The shimmering grandchildren of Grandpa Schein, dancing to the wry *schmaltz* of other Jewish immigrants in the Wasp-hallowed halls filled with the sacred relics of other ruling classes.

I *was* ashamed of my pride in it, but there it was, pride. Seldon Dochel had my number. He told me once, "You yak about social transformation, but you're pure burgher. Deep down you couldn't bear change. You'd be terrified you'd have to clean the toilets. That's what Blanqui said was the key question: 'Who'll empty the chamber pots?' "

True enough. Actually, my worst dreams are about drowning in shit. Jenny sent me some African novels; I couldn't bear them because every other page was about that. For me, the water closet stood with Opus 111 at the summit of culture. We Scheins, Firetucks, Glucks, and Riemers had long ago separated ourselves from filth, had, at least, translated it into our wallets—I accept the terrible equation between wealth and shit—into champagne, tuxedos, ebony men with gold fangs in their bellies. I looked on my relatives a bit distantly, like our cocker, snooty Verg, surveying our noisy dinners, but part of me danced along, spotlit with family pride, as if I too were in a lit-glass cage.

On Mother's eightieth birthday I gave her an album of old photographs, poems from the children, the front page of the *New York Times* the day of her birth. (Rumblings in Cuba, wheat deals in Chicago, "The Colored Race asks Protection in Railroad Discrimination.") Mrs. Brick and Mrs. Kraus, fellow corkscrewed veterans of the New York streets, came over. It was a wonderful couple of hours, with cake and champagne, six drops of which made her tipsy. At the end, she handed me an envelope of checks for everyone in the family, including Agnes, whose divorce from me ten years before had validated her distrust. ("She never says anything. Perhaps I should learn Polish." Agnes didn't know a word of Polish.) "Grandpa Schein used to say, 'When you get, give.' I was given. So I give."

A month later, walking in the icy streets, she stumbled, fell, and broke her arm. For a few months, this difficulty masked deeper ones. The fatigue, the pain, and the internal disorders were blamed on the bandaged arm. Her Sunday morning calls filled with self-accusation. "How could I be so stupid? I'm so clumsy. I've forgotten how to heal. I thought Lawrence would take off the bandage Thursday. It takes forever."

One Sunday there was no call. The calls had annoyed me for decades—nothing was said, just reassurance nothing catastrophic had happened. I waited two minutes, then telephoned her.

"Oh, son," said an oddly muffled voice. "How funny. I must've overslept." No, the arm hadn't healed yet.

The following Sunday, the phone was again silent. I called, and, in a voice that was scarcely heard, she managed to let me know that her mouth was full of sores.

"I use Akustak, Mother. I'm going to send you some."

No, she'd let Angelica, the maid, get it, how was it spelled? I spelled it twice, imagining her telling Angelica to write it down on the bedside pad with its handsome superscription: "RIEMER'S FINE MEATS. SINCE 1916."

I remember trying to go back to work. The April issue was due at the printer in two days, and I had to edit a piece about heat regulation in birds and reptiles. It was something sharp-eyed entrepreneurs could use. An easy piece, but it was giving me trouble. I went into the study and sat, not in my work chair, but on the upholstered pew facing Grandpa Riemer's butcher block and Grandpa Schein's patent for a spindle brake screw, the invention that underwrote so much of mother's ease. (And now underwrites mine.) Winged flywheels, vine-tangled trip-hammers, two sexless nude children holding the crimson stamp of the Viennese *Patentamt*. William Durant had bought the rights to it for a thousand shares of the company he was organizing; and what remained of that plurifying General Motors stock helped mother wash out the stigma of being the butcher's wife. "A Mother," I said aloud. "What is a mother?" I remembered waking at night, age—what?— five, six wanting her so badly, and, when she came, putting my cheek against hers, my arms around as much of her body as I could hold. These thousands of days later I could feel the silk scallops on the neck of that dress, the warm powder smell of her cheek, the tickle-comfort of her brown hair. For decades, we'd disagreed about almost every subject, every value, but those curls, those scallops, that fragrance, were in some safe place, deeper, safer, more truly *me* than any disagreement, any value.

In New York, a week before Mother died, I gave a party. My cousin, Jean Gluck, had a terrace penthouse on Ninety-first and Broadway. She was out of town, but two of her daughters were living it up there. They invited the young, I the middle-aged. They bought the liquor, supplied records, ordered cheese, corned beef, shrimp and French bread from Zabar's. The terrace was filled with hundreds of plants, the moon zipped up over the Palisades, the night was gold and emerald. I don't know the touchless dances of rock, but I danced. I don't drink well, but I drank. I talked nonsense, kissed people, and before I knew it, was asleep on a couch. When I woke, there was a shoe in my face. At its other end was a blond woman I didn't recognize. An hour later, we were having breakfast together. Vera was a talent scout, and invited me to go with her that night to Catch a Rising Star on Second Avenue to hear a rising comedian.

After my evening visit to Mother, I met her there. We sat in a packed room, drinking scotch. The comedian was a peach-cheeked boy with wide eyes and a terrible tongue. He worked over the audience, first a party of teenagers, then me. (The hangdog invitation in my face?) "Where you from, Mister?" I shook my head, to show I was not up to it. It would not do. This was his room, his time, his audience. He could not allow irresponse. If silence was all there was, he'd use it. "So shy? Such a tough-looking old guy, and so shy? Or maybe it's just Catatonics' Night Out at the asylum." I raised my hands in the gesture of helplessness. That was all I could do. If I'd been catatonic, it wouldn't have mattered. Cripple, cretin, Japanese, Jew, gimp, tramp, whore. Anything served. Any occupation was a useful minority: plumber, salesman, broker, geek. Man himself was a minority, something to work over. A Silent Guy, whether Dope, Drunk, Catatonic, or Mute, was tough material: but still material. And I, pointed out, publicized, was furious and stricken. He shook his head. "Where's the tongue, honey? Left it in the broad's tush?" The "broad" was mild, proper Vera. I pointed to my open mouth, jabbed for explanation: "I'm a mute. Can't talk," Or, "Cancer took my chords. Haven't learned laryngeal speech yet." Or, finally, "I'll play along another thirty seconds, but then get off my back."

To the audience (mostly kids, spending thirty bucks apiece): "These old fuckers are let in to fill the space of real people. They just plop there. Gray turds. Waiting to be wiped. Okay, Melvin"—to me—"the only thing you give away is your bad breath," and so on in the fecal, whorish patter of the rising stars of American nightclub comedy.

"I've got to go, Vera. This is not for me." I could hardly say that, I was on the verge of tears. What was I doing there with Mother taking the last breaths of her life? The comedian had smelled me out, he knew I shouldn't be in that audience.

On Second Avenue, I walked in crowds past restaurants and cafés, hundreds of places, all filled, all noisy. Thousands of automobiles, walkers, talkers, sitters, strollers, touchers; trillions of words, a hundred thousand jokes, a hundred thousand stories, come-ons, come-offs, getting found, getting lost. In this cauldron of entertainment, I'd been singled out for rebuke. Eighty-odd pounds of disintegrating flesh were going back into the earth, and their sole product had sat drinking in a spotlit room waiting for yuks. Sure, I'd been singled out. In my party-colored plaid and wrinkleless slacks, my white shirt and diamond-spotted blue tie, I stank of disharmony. If the galaxy had turned into a microscope, I would have been the perfect specimen of Out-of-Place.

Yet also I'd never felt so hungry for life. The streets, the movies, the park. Up on the roof with the kids waving their arms, snapping pelvises toward the shrubbery, spearing the shrimp, gobbling chunks of Brie-smeared French bread, the stars sneaking in through city lights, the Hudson pouring under the bridges, the red Palisades puckering up for New York. New York said, "Holy God, this is life."

Little mother, shrinking in her bed, knew it. When she stretched her head for my kiss, she croaked—her voice, never lovely, was now hoarse and metallic—"Have a good time, darling." Veteran of others' troubles, she knew hers would be survived. "Have a good time," she said when I left. And when I came in, "What have you been doing?"

I didn't tell her about the party. Sometimes I said I'd seen a movie. Or, "I've been walking. It's very hot. It's a relief to come in here."

I knew she knew it wasn't. She appreciated my lie. She appreciated *her son,* this burly, graying, balding person, who had grown so quickly from what had become her body and had given her so many now-forgotten pains (including a lifetime of gas attacks). I'd also given her grandchildren. The future. Not that she'd ever cared much for abstractions. It was the present that counted. She'd had no ambition. She'd wanted to live decently, to be respected, to have some fun. Good food, a few shows, ease, and *no trouble.* "Have a good time, darling."

I waited impatiently for her to die. The call from the hospital came at two in the morning. "In her sleep," said the nurse. "She was such a sweet lady."

"Thank you for everything," I said. I didn't wake my father.

Thirty hours later, I was in the uptown office of Mother's lawyer on the twentieth floor of the Chemical Bank building, part of midtown Park Avenue's glassy tunnel. Outside, reflections broke each other into abstractions of shimmer:

inside, crimson leather, bentwood rockers, golden love seats, knobbed and studded desks spelling domestic security and comfort.

Mother's lawyer; my lawyer. (There was pleasure in such an acquisition.) Ethan Crouse, dark-eyed, cherry-cheeked, thirty-five, a sharp, sympathetic face that could darken, turn severe. He described the will, we shifted to first names, he lost the age of his position, became younger, became mine. "There are no debts to speak of. You know your mother. It's straight and clear. No vaults, no safe deposit boxes. No real complexities. You're the heir and your father's trustee. It's an important estate, but fairly simple. I'll alert the banks and the accountant." I was in good hands. Very relaxing.

The only wrinkle came when I asked if we could discuss the fee. "Of course. That's a reasonable thing to do." Ethan's fingers interlaced, the face darkened. "Twenty-five thousand dollars should cover everything."

"Would you object if I investigated a bit further?"

"Not at all," said Ethan. "Makes a good deal of sense. I think you'll find this is the usual fee for an estate of this size. Perhaps smaller than some."

Two days later I called Ethan and said that I'd found a lawyer in a smaller firm who could handle the estate for fifteen thousand dollars. (I hadn't.)

Ethan said, "I think that's within our range. Since the estate is simple, I think we can manage to do it for that. If there are complications when it comes to your father's estate, we can discuss it later."

"Fine," I said, dismissing what I too grandly—if correctly—assumed would be my father's brief tenure.

Mother would have been proud of me: I'd saved ten thousand dollars.

* * *

The next morning, in one of Campbell's funeral Lincolns, we drove up the Hudson into Westchester, Dad, Angelica, Mrs. Kraus, and Mrs. Brick. Ahead was the hearse with the steel box within which lay the small body. The Riemer plot was up a green slope. Angelica and I helped Dad walk. We'd explained the occasion to him thirty times. He was silent now, his lovely eyes either uncertain or dodging certainty. Tiny Mrs. Brick strode to the head of the coffin. I read, " 'As the hart panteth after the water brooks, so panteth my soul after thee, O God. My tears have become my meat day and night while they continually say unto me, "Where is thy God?" Why art thou cast down, O my soul; and why art thou disquieted in me. . . . Deep calleth unto deep at the noise of the waterspout: all thy waves and thy billows have gone over me. Why art thou cast down, O my soul? And why art thou disquieted within me.' Good-bye, dear Mother."

Angelica, who expected more of a service, supplied it herself, kneeling and reciting, " 'The Lord is my shepherd, I shall not want.' "

Mrs. Brick said, "God bless you, Naomi." She lay three red roses on the coffin.

Dad whispered to me, "Who is it, Cyrus? Who is the poor soul?" Angelica led him back to the car.

I walked up the slope and stood among the trunks of live oak. Beyond the black Lincoln glittered marble sarcophagi; beyond them, silvery bits of the Hudson flashed through branches. Crickets whacked away, birds asserted themselves. The expensive memorial hill shone with lost life.

1 1 1

When I lost what made me a son—for Dad died in Angelica's arms eight weeks to the hour after Mother—I got what made me rich. Rich compared to what I'd been, not rich on the scale of the Duke of Westminster. (Sixteen thousand dollars an hour, I read in the *Wall Street Journal*, wondering if that included the hours of sleep; I suppose the Duke, like me, now, could sleep and earn at once.) Not even rich on the scale of the poorest millionaire, but rich enough to change my life and, it turned out, the way I thought.

Someone said being happy was having what one needed and needing what one had. I've been a happy fellow. As for money, it altered my needs more than my possessions. It also altered the way I appeared to others.

Before I became an heir, I'd been in various anterooms of

money. Comfortable, knowing it wasn't far away, yet delighted that I needed very little of it, and that I could think—did think—I didn't give a damn about it. Oh, it was important, but almost more as a subject than a need. Reading pieces by my old contributor Mel Sorgmund, I could work up an interest in it. God—or at least Mel—knows it is complex. It has its own physics as well as its own psychology. There is money ethics and money esthetics. There is a monetary pennant race, there are monetary wars; in the monetary universe old solidities—coal, wheat, steel, tractors—ricochet and sometimes shatter on a financial Van Allen Belt—Ginnie Maes, Fanny Maes, Freddie Macs, CD's, T-notes, calls, puts, repos, options, futures. In the romance of money, dollars chased each other, chased yen, chased gold, chased guesses about where they'd be. Mel was one of the great exegetes of this world, and over the decade I watched him become one of its prophets, one of its gods. Like God, he had time for everything, so he kept on sending the *News-Letter* a few pages while great magazines, corporations, and nations paid him enormous fees and flew him in company and national jets to boardrooms, ministries, and conferences. Mel had leapt from writing technical analyses in economic journals to the analysis of any social phenomenon that came his way. The cost of bananas, the cost of freedom, Mel explained both. He told newspaper readers why countries went down the drain and answered those who said he'd sent them there by saying that the politicians hadn't taken *all* his advice. "Anyway," he said with his wonderful smile—huge as a Halloween pumpkin's though subtilized by an old scar-fold in the upper lip—"I'm ahead. I've sunk fewer than I've saved." Sorgmundites—any literate reader knew what this meant—bankrolled a television series which featured little Mel paddling down Bangkok klongs (to explain barter), jeeping into astonished

African villages, casting lines into Canadian rivers ("Nature's exhaustible bounty"), instructing ancient pensioners in Fort Lauderdale, bankers in Zurich, dictators in Santiago, and presidents in the White House. A philosophy, a government, a grocery store, a pension plan—they were all grist for Mel. The world was full of systems and enterprises which had been deformed by non-Sorgmundites but that with Sorgmundian medicine—it was always bitter—could be reformed. Herblock drew him as Christ in the Last Judgment between those saved by Sorgmundian grace and damned by un-Sorgmundized ignorance.

"What should I do with my dough, Mel?" I asked him.

Mel had spent the afternoon working out an indexing system for Argentina. "My guess is to leave it where it is. I mean, I can tell you a few tricks, Cy—borrowing from your broker to the value of your securities, investing it in real estate and cutting the interest out of your taxes—but what the hell. That's not for you. You're like me. Money isn't real unless your hands and brains earned it. You and I don't have the right temperament for speculation. I haven't made a nickel in the market. Don't have the time, don't have the interest. Neither one of us really gives a damn about money." I wish readers of financial pages could have heard this.

Still, I did give a damn about it. I even altered my habits. I bought better cigars and paid eight dollars for wine instead of three. I didn't hesitate about buying records. I sent the children bigger birthday and Christmas checks. I didn't stew over sales and bargains, though it still gave me a thrill to save a buck at a drugstore. Frugality and abstemiousness were part of me. The new pleasures floated above them. The chief pleasure was accumulation, the surprise of it, the dividend checks coming out of the financial blue, the little savagery of proprietary delight. When I used the

phone, I'd find myself thinking, "I own some of you, Ma Bell. I'm paying myself when I use you." That I should own a few molecules of the telephone, of the gasoline in my old Malibu's tank, dazzled me. DuPont, Exxon, Union Carbide, Commonwealth Edison, they too were now *mine*. I understood how one could be a Republican. I tried to separate myself from the feelings behind this understanding, tried to think I was amused by this money-enlarged Riemer striding along with people I'd spent much of my life despising. I said to Emma, "What did I do to have what I have? Should I sleep easy because Grandpa Schein had an idea a quarter century before I was born?"

"But you don't sleep easy," she said. "It's as if every dollar's dropped a piece of lead in your skull. Why not just enjoy it? Why should it be a problem for you?"

"It won't let you enjoy it. It doesn't just sit there. It's got a life of its own. Even if you only take it to the bank, even if you have it sent to the bank, there's a deposit slip. Even if I got you to manage it, or Merrill Lynch, somewhere there'd be a reckoning with it. It gets up and tells you what to do. Want it or not, it's out there, chugging away, swelling up. It burns holes in your pockets. It burns holes in other people's pockets. You know the mail I get, the phone calls. I'm part of a network. It's enough to make one feel sorry for Rockefeller. The more bucks, the more strings. Gulliver tied down. Repos, CD's, tax-free municipals, depreciations, cattle, timber, machinery, real estate, minerals. This stuff is not simple. And I'm not talking about deciding whether to buy this or sell that. I can feel it taking root in my nature. *Depreciation.* There's a deep conception there. Heidegger should have looked at that. Some tax sharpie decided everything that exists is threatened, so if you shelter it, you save it and are entitled to payment for your good deed. I hate it. I'm afraid of it. But I'm afraid to give it up. And I hate whatever's in my nature that's afraid to give it up. Wittgenstein gave away his money."

"So did Saint Francis," said Emma. "But you're only little Fay."

Thousands and thousands of less philosophic intelligences burned with plans for my money. For the first time in my life, I read the financial pages. Sometimes I even bought the *Wall Street Journal*. I found myself calling 800 numbers for the day's gold price, the quotations for pork bellies, treasury notes, the balance in my mutual fund.

I also acquired—this seemed to be the new verb in my life—a broker. I answered an ad about municipal bonds in the financial section of the *New York Times* and four days later was telephoned by one Billy Jugiello of Cockroft and Venim.

Billy had a comfortable voice, baritone, unpressured, vaguely southern. He called me "Doctor."

"Good morning, Doctor, it's Billy. Something just came down the pike here I think's gonna interest you."

I never laid eyes on him, but he became a presence for me. He called two or three times a week. I imagined him as a big fellow. On the morning news show I started to watch, there was a man who did the weather, a 250-pounder with a chin like a plant pot, pig-bright eyes, ox shoulders, no neck; he was beautifully tailored and wore carnations in his buttonhole. This was the person I saw when I talked to Billy.

"One day," Emma told me, "you'll go down to his office and find out he's a dwarf."

"Never. I won't go. I've got to believe he's substantial."

"Good morning, doctor. It's B——"

"Hello, Billy, what's up?"

"Had a call from New York. There's a blip in the money market and we've put together a batch of municipals at

eleven-point-three-six. Want to move about twenty thousand into it?"

For months, the odd excitement was that there was so
little excitement in that amount of money. The money was
as abstract as a quark's charm. Or not quite. Money waited
to swim up the fallopian tubes of Cockroft and Venim
where, with slightly more chance than the average sperma-
tozoon, it could compound another magical abstraction.

"How much do we have in municipals?"

I imagined him punching out his chart on a glass screen.
"Seventy-five thousand."

"What the hell. Buy twenty-five. It'll give us an even
hundred grand." (This was not the editorial-papal-royal *us*.
It was the oligarchical, conspiratorial *us*.) "Less for Uncle."
We knew who Uncle was. The enemy. The IRS. The
slippery stinger, Uncle Sam. I was in the forty-six percent
bracket, and, to my amazement, found myself sympathiz-
ing with some of the worst types in the history of inhuman-
ity, greedy porkers whose mental life was consumed in
schemes of avoidance. Their lives were used up trying to
save greater percentages of their whiskey, their boats, the
cells in their wives' and children's bodies, their own dollar-
ized and dolorous hearts. Taxation was theft, the official
theft of Washington's second-story men (who otherwise
spent their time churning out ever more useless paper.) And
I was with them. "The only capital that counts for us
neanderthals is what doubles itself. It has about as much
relation to thirst, hunger, warmth or sex as a car's paint to
its motor." "It's still poetry for you, Cy," said Emma.
"That's what inoculates you."

"I wanna tell you about something else, Doctor. A guy in
the next office has a pipeline to Central America. You know
about Mexican oil?"

"I know they have plenty of it."

"There's only one company listed on the Exchanges connected to it." Jugiello strangled some Spanish name. "It's got exclusive rights to Mexican tubing. Builds all the pipes down there. It's selling at eight. Up a quarter yesterday. This is solid. It has to go up. It couldn't hurt to get three or four hundred shares. Just put it away and forget it. I'm gonna pick up a couple of hundred shares for myself."

"All right, Billy. Pick it up." (The next month Tubos Mexicana de Açero slid to three, where it stayed till I sold it.)

"What about a good fiber-optic, Billy? I've got a CD coming through next week."

I felt I was one of Jugiello's favorite clients, felt he respected my limited interest in sheer acquisition. Wasn't I really interested in finding out how business worked? I read company reports, thought about the meaning of market blips and industrial trends. I was Columbus, not Pizarro; Ricardo, Marx, and Sorgmund, not Morgan, Rockefeller, and Rothschild. It was knowledge, not dough and power, that got me.

At Christmas, he sent me a grotesque card of incised ivy and purple roses on which was printed, "Greetings from Billy and Priscilla Jugiello."

"Jugiello's married," I told Emma.

"Don't be too sure. Priscilla might be the Chicago office of Tubos Mexicana."

Was Billy freckled? Spastic? I knew only that he had a B.A. from Lansing, and that what I knew, he didn't. (And vice versa.) When he heard I edited a science newsletter, I could hear his teeth hit the phone. (The doctor stuff came from that.) He told me he had to be very careful talking with me. "Is that the right word, Doctor?" he'd ask. "Have

I used that word right?" (The word was *infinitesimal*.) "There'd be an infinitesimal advantage," he said. "Is *infinitesimal* right, Doctor? I mean just a tiny bit of advantage. I don't mean it to be infinite. Right?" Touching. Yet I felt him selling something all the time. Even when he sounded as if he was on his death bed. " 'Ocho, Doctor."

"What's the matter, Billy?"

"I feel lousy."

"Go on home."

"Don't want the boss to think I'm ducking out."

All these bird verbs of default: chickening out, ducking out. "What's the market doing?"

"I've got a tip for you."

"Your tips are disasters, Billy."

A croak that served for a laugh, "Gwaan, Doctor. We only had a few little mistakes. Tubos Mex, Neo-Bionics. Hershey too, I think. But don't forget Marathon. We did all right on that one, didn't we?"

"We made up a little ground on that one, right."

"Want to buy three hundred more?" A sneeze, undeflected from the phone. I imagined three hundred pounds convulsing, shaking the computers a hundred yards away. (Or was the invisible croaker a runt?) "Actually, the market's up eleven points."

A blip in my heart. How easily money's made. (Though not by the thousands who built the brake with grandpa's screw.) The sun hit the bricks outside. More easy gold. I'll give Benedict a Riemer Fellowship to work on his book. And trade in Rufus (the Malibu). I'll think of something for Emma, Livy, Jenny; and Jack too; even something for Agnes. Bless her heart. Bless Jugiello too. "You're a prince, Billy. Let's have news like this every week."

"I'd love it, Doctor. No more Tubos Mex. Fac' is, I got

something you should look at." I said nothing, just tightened around the Jugiello risk. "A friend of mine—this is not from New York, this is my own—this friend's cousin's connected with this company that's got this new process for making a urinalysis. It's a question of—I'm no scientist now—it's got something to do with a microscope that does the analyzing direct so you don't have to send it to the lab. Like a Polaroid. On the spot you see it. You know how many urinalyses are made in the United States alone? My God, it's a gold mine. Liquid gold." Another croaking rumble of ha-has. "I been buying it myself. It's at five now. My gut feeling is it'll be at forty before the year's out."

"Where can I follow it, Billy?"

"Doctor, take my word for it. Don't follow it. It's at—let's see—five and a quarter today, up a quarter from yesterday. Buy a thousand shares and put it away. What can you lose?"

"What I always lose. You haven't even told me the name."

"Orchisonics. It's got something to do with sound waves. It's listed under Additional Over the Counter. Only in the *Journal*. Trust me, doctor. Remember Marathon."

"I'll let you know, Billy."

I didn't trust Billy, but somehow I liked him, and more, wanted to be liked by him. The next time he called—and he always called within a day of mentioning a stock—I bought a thousand shares of Orchisonics.

What am I worth?

Saturday, I go out for the newspaper and bring it to the desk, where, pushing back galleys, periodicals, reference books, and graphs, I take out of my money drawer white sheets I've ruled into columns of rectangles. Down the left side are the names of my twenty-four stocks with their prices on the day I inherited or bought them. In adjacent columns I write the market quotations of the Friday closures. With a five-dollar calculator (a premium from the savings and loan in the days when I kept my few dollars there) I multiply shares by price. Into the grass-green slot appear, lit up, the perforated figures.

MARKET CLOSE	Aug 12	Aug 19	Aug 21
	886.16	893.47	887.91
19¼			
490 shares	$8820	$9001	$8697
AmEl P	18	18³/₈	17³/₄
52¼			
650 shares	$36,400	$36,725	$36,400
AT&T	56	56½	56
55			
60 shares	$3540	$3427	$3405
AT&T pf.	59	57⅛	56³/₄
22³/₈			
100 shares	$2013	$2075	$2037
CWE	20⅛	20³/₄	20³/₈
31			
300 shares	$10,800	$11,175	$11,434
DUP	36	37¼	38⅛

And so on.

The final luxury's addition. Though the result is twenty times what I could have listed as my total worth four years ago, the figure no longer delights me. Nor would it if I added the bonds (too difficult to look up), treasury notes, or the cash in money funds (one swelling at a hundred dollars a week, the other—a new "aggressive" fund I'd heard about on "Wall Street Week"—at double that). More than a nest egg, it's a viable, flyable bird.

Yet there is a small pain that I'm not a millionaire.

In the last quarter of the twentieth century, a million American dollars is, on this side of the tracks, not that impressive. Good welterweights split fifteen million for thirteen three-minute rounds. Fifteen or twenty tennis players clear a quarter to a half a million dollars a year; three or four make eight million. Every day, executives, actresses, ball players, "anchor persons," sign multiyear contracts for multimillions of dollars. One in every four or five hundred Americans is a millionaire.

I wanted to be one too. An absurd ambition, like, say, wanting to be the best-dressed obstetrician in Albany or the sexual prince of Tucson, but there it was.

My worth.

All right, I knew it couldn't be answered by the six lit figures in the calculator slot, but still, that worth, quantifiable, calculable, rulable, writable, was not merely a time filler on Saturday morning. It stood for—in a way *is*—what nothing else in my life is, something absolute, something comparable. On most worldly graphs it stands for achievement, power, comfort, arrival, security. (On other graphs, those drawn by theorists of distribution and rage, it stands for shame, for the theft of other people's energy.) One way or another, it signified a perspective of the soul. It made certain things worthless, even harmful, *sin*ful. Or it said, "You belong. You've made it. You are someone who counts." Who *counts*.

It got so that if stocks were up, then so was I. When they were down, it was gloom-and-doomsville. Six months after mother's death, the market went into a tailspin. I panicked.

I got out my charts and saw I was thirty thousand dollars poorer than I'd been a week ago. Even when I hadn't known how I'd pay the next printer's bill I wasn't so panicked. "What's going on down there, Billy?"

"The bears are eatin' honey an' makin' money, Doc."

"I'm not. When is this going to end?"

"There's always an end, Doc."

That wasn't what I needed. I wanted advice, wisdom, assurance. "What are you doing with your own dough, Billy?"

"I live by eighths and sixteenths, Doc. I buy and sell every hour. That isn't for you. You don't need cash, do you?"

"I can buy groceries today. That doesn't mean I want smoke in my portfolio."

"Doc, I'm ready to sell, just say the word."

But *the word* is what I wanted from him. I felt very much alone. I thought of calling Seldon, but Seldon never *talked* business with me, only let his gloom about it run over our post-tennis juice and muffins. Maybe Jack would know something. In all his time at Dochel and Moshur's, I'd never visited him.

"Jack, feel like having a little lunch with me? I thought I'd pay you a visit."

"What a surprise, Dad. I'll take you down to the Floor if you like. It's a terrific scene, you'll love it."

"I just want to see you. I'm lonely. I could use your advice too. This market's upsetting me."

I took the I.C. downtown and walked over on Jackson to the Board of Trade building. Jack was waiting for me at the newsstand in a navy blazer. I felt proud of him. In the lobby crowd, he looked like he belonged, a real man.

We went to a hamburger joint under the el-tracks and sat

across from each other in a leather booth. There was protective comfort there. The light was low and made for intimacy, to which we gave body service, leaning toward each other. "Are things as bad in commodities as they are in the stock market?" I asked.

"It's different, but they're lousy. I lost a couple of thousand myself."

"I didn't know you had that much to lose. Or is it Maria's dough?"

"Hell no. All mine. Or rather, all not-mine. I made it, I lost it. You still think I'm a punk."

"Of course I don't."

"I am. I thought I knew what I was doing. I watched Felix and followed right behind. You'd think after all these months here I'd know you can't play unless you have real money. Or guts. I was scared, and I blew it."

Then he must have remembered he was the counselor, not the frightened son. His face tightened. "It's a lousy time, Dad. I'd get out of the market. Get cash. Put it in a bank or under your mattress."

"Is that what people are saying? Moshur? Seldon?"

"They don't care. They make money up or down. As long as there is money, they make it. If there's a crash, then there's nothing. I think that's what's happening now. We're near the end of the line."

There Jack was, soft-cheeked with his unsettled gray eyes, poor teeth, onion-heavy breath, and years of mistakes and easy ways out. "I wouldn't toot the last trump too quickly, Jack. Panic's when real money men clean up."

"You never think I know anything."

With a crescent of hamburger juice on his lip, he looked as he did age seven, caught out in some fib. Metamorphosis. While back in the Exchange, bulls were losing horns, growing shag and selling what they'd been grazing. What an Ovidian world. "Of course I do. I must have seen my own panic in you. It put me off."

"I mean what's the point of asking, if you don't care what I say?"

The father makes the child childish. "Jack, I'm sorry. Take it easy. I don't mean to question your expertise."

"I'm no expert, you know that. It's just another put-down. Your opinion counts for *me*. You sounded worried, I told you what I think. I don't put out a financial letter. It's my gut feeling."

"And I appreciate it. We're both on edge."

"Are you in trouble? You look unsteady."

"I'm fine. You should be so fine. I'm just edgy. I've lost a little dough, that's all. I never had any before. I don't know how to handle it. I was thinking I could just coast to the grave. This is a good lesson for me. Get me off my duff. It's time to think of something new. I've still got energy." I did just then, and my tongue ran away. "You won't be burying me for a while. I hope that doesn't disappoint you."

"That's not funny." The little face chugged with anger and pout.

A little too much reaction, I thought, but I better zip my lip. "Sorry again. I can't say anything right today." He put a hand on my sleeve and patted it. "I'm proud of you, Jack. You've really stuck it out down here." The filial-fatherly hand slid off. "You may have lost a few bucks, but you've gained an awful lot."

"What?"

"I don't know."

"I'm not getting anywhere here. Maria's soaring, that's great, but all I do is make and lose other people's dough. This isn't what life's about."

"I wouldn't want you here forever."

"I get up, look at my watch, it's seven-thirty. I go in the kitchen, make my coffee, seven-thirty-five. I shave, I dress, it's ten of eight. Two minutes after eight, I catch the el. Everybody's checking his watch, the watches are all the same."

"Well, that's the world. I mean you can go to Tahiti and live by sun and moon time."

"Why not live by inside clocks?"

"Fair enough. Look, I just upset you, coming down here, busting in with my little no-troubles."

"No," he said. "This is the highlight of the month. That's what gets me. That it should be the highlight."

I walked back to the I.C. through the crowd. I felt like the ruined speculator in Antonioni's *L'Eclisse* walking out of the Roman Borsa (in which the pillars of an old temple are stuck like stone ghosts); he tears up his trade slips and drops them in the street; it's all over; no one notices him. No one noticed me. Thousands of human monads circulating in a white dazzle. Me. Jack. What to do, where to go?

The country was drowning in money. Like old Spain, glutted with New World gold, just before it began its four-hundred-year-long nose-dive. Inflation, aggression, craziness. U.S. of A. *Us*. And what was *us?* Forty million crimes, forty million illiterates, two million runaway and kidnapped kids, millions out of work, fifty million crazies. And the rest of us slobbering with greed and fear.

Maybe they'd already dropped the bomb, only it was invisible, silent.

For the first time in my life, I found myself thinking, What the hell, who needs this? Maybe it's time to tune up for the Big Zero. Then I'd walk to the lake, or read a book, or just hear someone hammering in the courtyard below. I'd study a hornet drumming at the window or remember the little lump on Livy's nose. And I'd pull back. Not quite ready for Nowheresburg.

Seeing me clunk around, Emma would sink herself. "Dump me, Cy. Get yourself a fresh trick." (I didn't have the energy to even consider that.) Then she'd mope around till she found *her hornet*. A new slogan would go up on the red heart—*Viva Vendredi*—she'd turn merry, obscene, and that would haul me back.

Life still had surprises up its sleeve. (Sometimes it seemed all sleeve.) My college roommate and oldest friend, Burleigh Fulmer, got married for the fourth time. I saw Burleigh once or twice a year. He'd come see me to get material for his program. (He filmed four-minute chunks of information, advice, and moral caution—he was the informer, adviser, and cautioner—and sold them to television stations, which used them for their public service obligation at six in the morning.) Burleigh had come quite a way from a Galesburg farm and Knox College. Which was another reason he came to see me. To let me know how far he'd come. I'd been editor of the Knox paper, a junior Phi Bete and, though no Brando, had done all right with coeds. Burleigh was an awkward, lumpy hayseed. He was still awkward but, wrapped in a good suit and gleaming with his dour television authority, he looked all right. He'd park his Porsche in front of Rufus, my rusting heap, and hang his six-hundred dollar Capper and Capper overcoat over my stained parka. I didn't mind offering my financial inferiority to Burleigh, even when it no longer existed. (It was an inexpensive gift, and he was a decent fellow under his sour puss and moralizing chirp.) His new wife was a diminutive Colombian lady with a name all vowels. She was hardly bigger than a wart on Burleigh's bulk. "Why not you and Emma make twosome wedding weet us?"

"That's a wonderful idea, Biduaya," I said, "but Burleigh does all the marrying here." Dancing around with Emma in Burleigh's Lake Shore condo, I was happily swacked. Once, Burleigh had to pick me off the floor.

"Bidu's right, Cy," he said. "Weddings are great things. Cake, champagne, pals, preachers, ceremony, sacrament, the law. A few sentences, and you go home doubled. Twice the person you were."

"I've been married."

"Not often enough."

Bidu's tiny finger shook at Burleigh. "Thees last one for you, beeg boy."

"One never do know, do one, Cy? You sure you and Emma don't want in? Bargain rates."

"We're happy throwing your rice, Burleigh."

It was not the only wedding of the summer.

Jack called. "We were looking at Charles and Diana's wedding. The two of them kind of lost-and-found in the middle of that hoopla. And something clicked in us."

I too had waked in the dark and watched the royal wedding. The throng in Saint Paul's had been turned by the camera into a living rose window. The bride's train, an enormous dragonfly wing, had bisected it. I lay in bed drinking coffee and spreading strawberry jam in the toasted curls of English muffin. An Australian soprano with a Maori name sang an English aria by a German composer. The groom said, "With *thy* worldly goods I thee endow," and the bride got his six names mixed up. Eternal troth was sanctified before divorcees on both sides of the aisle. I thought, "We're the kings here, eating our muffins while the actors entertain us." (But later, down in Greensboro—where Jack and Maria were married at her grandmother's house—I realized television royalty doesn't count. Too passive. Too remote.)

"We were drinking Gatorade at the kitchen table," said Jack. "Then we went jogging. While they drove back to Buckingham Palace. Our running shoes were stinking up the kitchen. We just kind of looked at each other, sweating away. It was very serious. 'Shall we?' I think I said it. So we kissed each other, like the end of a forties movie."

"Maybe a Riemer gene is triggered by something holy. Anyway, I'm delighted for you. It isn't a matter of pregnancy then?"

"If you mean *is Maria?* No. We haven't said a word about kids."

"Wish you'd say a few," I said. "I'm a great lover of the creatures."

"Be a do-it-yourself grandpa then. You're not over the hill. And Emma's not all that much older than Maria."

"I've had three decades with you guys. I don't have another three decades to give a kid of my own. But a grandchild would sweeten my life no end."

"I hope I'll sweeten it someday, Dad."

"Sorry, Jack. I've got no right to talk like this. I'm delighted for you and Maria. Let's have a great wedding."

"You and Emma want to make it a double?"

The world seemed to be concerned about our getting hitched. "No, we've worked out a way of living. Marital cement might drag us under." Why did people regard marriage as a certificate of good behavior? "But I'm glad you're getting hitched. Because of children."

"Doesn't Emma want to marry?"

"Sometimes."

"Doesn't she want a kid?"

"She has two. Herself and me."

Jack's wedding was the first family gathering since my father's funeral (though only two Schein cousins and no other Riemers came). Maria planned and produced it. A big job. The logistics included meeting people on planes flying in from seven states and putting them in houses and motels. The wedding itself took place in her grandmother's Carolina garden.

Emma didn't go. "They don't really want me."

"Of course, they do. Your name's on the invitation."

"I appreciate that, tell Maria, but this isn't the time to meet Agnes."

"If you think so," I said. (Relieved.)

In the garden, there was a grand, peppermint-striped tent. In it, a ten-piece orchestra. (Maria had worked out deals with everybody, caterers, violinists, the preacher.)

It was the archaeology that touched me: the strata of life stirred and reassembled. The beauty of a group, which, at such a time, slides over meanness. The paraphernalia: the white dresses, the champagne, the music, the abundance. Memories and catching up. That was the occasion's soul: the dead remembered, the living in full dress. Survival, success, celebration, ceremony.

Maria was one of the few girls in her college class who'd married. A year ago, the class president had issued a questionnaire and sent out the results. Of fifty girls, only six had married; of these, four were divorced. Next to "Marital Status," Maria had written, "Not married to Jack Riemer." (Her maid of honor, Robin Tuck, said she was "formerly not married to Walter Schneyer," and, before that, "wasn't married to Skipper LaPointe.") Now here was Maria, the sweet ideologist of porn, all lacy and white, surrounded by bridesmaids in beautiful old dresses that had been picked up around the country by Mama Pengratz, a brilliant canvasser of thrift shops. This white cloud of girls floated downstairs on the Lohengrin March to a terrace of gold and crimson roses. Jack, engulfed in a morning coat, looked stunned. His eyes seemed to be attending some other ceremony. Beside him was Ben; in front, Maria's cousin Thomas, a Jesuit, dressed in a floor-length black frock with red satin buttons from ankle to neck, like somebody in a Carpaccio fresco. He read from 1 Corinthians about putting away the things of a child and seeing through a glass darkly, a passage about which the groom was led to say to me ten minutes later, "Wasn't that beautiful? My God, that guy is a genius."

"Who?"

"Tommy. The guy in the weird outfit who married us. He is some writer."

"You should see the bit he wrote about 'the Lord is my shepherd.' That's really the bee's knees."

"What do you mean?"

"I mean I've neglected your spiritual education."

But this was no time for anything but high spirits. Surrounded by congratulators, Jack was delirious. I, too.

Among the children, their friends and cousins, in the garden with the girls in white, listening and telling stories, updated, edited, revised, polished and, above all, washed in fresh attention, I felt terrific. After the reception line, champagne in hand, I buzzed around the garden. It was full of dogwood—it was the dogwood that had brought the wedding to North Carolina. Stony with Chicago and starved for flowers, I gorged on it.

A girl in dogwood colors, pink and white with stains of green, came up. More than six feet, she was inches taller than I. She asked if I remembered her.

"I've never known anyone as splendid as you."

"You're the same gallant man."

She had a long, solemn face backed by a foot and a half of dark red hair. I touched it. "I think I do remember the color of this."

"I'm Nancy Triplett. You published my first piece in the *News-Letter*. I was so ignorant I sent in a picture. I thought maybe you'd remember."

"Of course. That amazing piece about menstrual cycles in the dormitory." I hadn't known the piece was by a college student. She'd observed that the menstrual cycles of cloistered women tended to converge. The picture of the girl with red hair came with a one-line biography—"Junior at Wellesley College." Amazed, I'd sent the piece to a biologist at the university to be checked out, and I published it. Six months later, she'd called me up, and we had coffee on the terrace of the Café Procope. "I've blocked you out," I said. "I never got over publishing something by someone so young. It was a wonderful piece. I'm sure you've done many since, but I haven't kept up."

"No," she said. "I went on for a couple of years, even published a couple of other things. Then it stopped. I didn't have it anymore. I drove a taxi in New York. I took poetry classes at Columbia. I hung around with the saddest junkie in Manhattan. Then I did a couple of movies for Mr. Robusto. That's how I got to know Maria. Now I go around to my friends' weddings—Mr. Robusto paid my way— hoping something nice is going to happen to me. Now it just did."

"I hope you mean the dogwood. Because if I'm the nicest thing that's happened to you, you are in a bad way."

"Well, you are," she said. "It's partly what you stand for for me. I was so much better off when you took me to that wonderful place under the blue awning, and we talked about nematods and gene gradients and bithorassic flies. All the confidence I had then. But I couldn't hack it. Nobody in my family has ever hacked it." The dogwood put pink shadows on her cheeks. Her eyes had a kind of Picasso-black intensity and brilliance. "I come from a long line of mongrel bitches who married a long line of con men. I don't know why I like coming to these things."

Not for a long time had an attractive confessional spigot been turned on for me; and I sensed it wasn't just nostalgia that stirred Nancy. But where did that put me, there in my *Paterfamilias* outfit among the wedding guests? "Anybody who could do at twenty what you did isn't out of it. You're years shy of thirty, you haven't even started yet. You don't have to live out anybody else's melodramas. Look at all this terrific human fruit here. Go pick yourself an apple. Cheer up. You're a wonderful girl. I'm going to get you some champagne." I stretched to kiss her cheek, pointed a champagne tray her way, and went over to intoxicate myself with more tranquil drafts. Side by side, in fuzzy white and silk dresses, were Livy and Robin. Like sisters a bit, though Livy was more stolid, rosier. Robin's face was calmer, unfissured by—what was it?—subtlety, worry, lack of confidence? She was a balladeer; Livy had sent me some of her poems. "I showed Robin *your* old poems, Dad. She thought they were wonderful. Maybe you could give her a few tips."

Astonishing that for a few years I'd thought of myself as a poet. I'd published maybe ten poems in the Stuyvesant and Knox literary magazines and three of four more the year I worked for the City News Bureau.

"When are we gonna see a volume from you, Mr. Riemer?"

"A volume? It'd be a mighty small one, Robin. Lots of white pages, twelve short poems."

"What a waste. I think you write like an angel. Maybe a fallen one. One who's seen everything bright and has to tell about it before he hits the ground."

"At my best, I was never close to that, Robin."

"You still write wonderfully. Livy shows me the *News-Letter*. The editorials are beautiful."

Even in this garden and on such an occasion, I was uneasy with compliments. You were made a knight with a sword: a half-inch turn, and it cut you. "I may not be doing the *Letter* much longer, Robin. Maybe I'll put out a sort of anthology and call it quits. I'm running out of steam."

"Sure, I can see *that*, Mr. Riemer. You look younger than the groom. Come stay with Livy a bit. I'm gonna pick up your other son. I haven't seen him since he's grown a beard. He's gorgeous. No time like a wedding to get me thinking. If no one'll marry me, at least I'm gonna get kissed." She went over to Benedict, who seemed to be bowing under the charms of Nancy Triplett.

"You should take your shot at all this, Livy." The colors of everything—floral, arboreal, sartorial—churned in a rainbow stew. Bridesmaids, honeysuckle, lobster, oranges, champagne, silver, sun, shadow. Everything was colored by everything else. Even the blue sky leaned down like a family friend. "I don't want you wasting yourself on your old pa." But it was lovely on the bench beside her, she in sunlight, me in the dogwood's blue shadow. "Though stay a minute or two. I see so little of those I love. Christmas. Weddings. Maybe, one of these days, yours."

Her face, so jolly and eager, drew in a bit and crimsoned. Livy, a mass of disposable feeling, was a great blusher. Fluent, even garrulous, on emotional occasions—for her there were many— she couldn't talk. The night before, at the prenuptial dinner—we'd taken over a downtown restaurant—Ben, Jenny, and even Agnes had supplied comic and sentimental histories of Jack. (I'd been toastmaster, noisy, looped, interrupting with horselaughs and irrelevant anecdotes.) Livy had gotten up to "summarize"—she'd managed to say—"the history of Jack as older brother." After four sentences, her voice broke, she blushed scarlet, and tears ran down. This was the girl who handcuffed men double her weight, spent half her days with thieves, brawlers, and killers, who chivvied lawyers, shook down agencies and did more difficult good in a month than I in my life.

"Nothing on that horizon, Dad. I intimidate people."

"Nonsense."

But it wasn't. Now and then, Livy would call me late at night—after ten-thirty for me—and I'd ask, "Is anything wrong?" a hangover from my mother's sense that the phone was for emergencies. "No." Her light voice would be hoarse with embarrassment. "Just feeling lonely. My murderer's back in jail."

"Haseltier?" I knew her cast of characters.

Or almost. "Haselmeier."

"The one who stuffed his cousin in the meat grinder? The one who has twenty 'I love mom's' on his thing?"

"The cousin turned up. In one piece. Haselmeier's not as bad as he talks."

"I wish you had better company, sweetie. Isn't Mrs. Fruehauf around?" She was only a thief. "Or what's-his-name, the cop you like?"

"Fister. Both on vacation."

"Well, you take one and come up here. Stay with me."

Emma, coming in in her shortie yellow nightgown, got the last of this. "Who're you inviting? Brooke Shields?"

"It's Livy."

"I'm saving up my time," said Livy. "You know I've got my application into the Bureau." It was her second try for the FBI. It softened the whole government for me to think of Livy in J. Edgar Hoover's chair. "Love to Emma, Dad. Bye-bye."

I felt her loneliness doubled by my having Emma. Once I suggested she come up so I could introduce her to a new contributor, a biochemist at Northwestern. "I wouldn't be able to open my mouth," she said. "There's too much to those people. The dumbest people are too complicated for me."

Now, under the dogwood, she said, "Maybe I ought to try harder. It's so nice here, the first time we've all been together for so long. I'm so glad Jenny and Oliver are back. I wish he could have come down for this. But you look a little shaky to me, Dad. Is it seeing all of us? I mean, seeing us growing a little out of reach?"

"Oh, no, Liv-heart, I'm in good shape. Grandma didn't name me Cyrus for nothing. Conquests left and right. I think Grandma and Grandpa's deaths hit me harder than I'd guessed they would. And her money's given me a rough time. I know it sounds silly, your clients should have such trouble. But it's made my little world spin around. There were all those years just getting by. We always did, and I liked that, but now there's—what can I say?—this superfluity. It makes you feel full one day and empty the next. You have the pleasure of getting something, and then you feel guilty. At least I do. I was such a high-minded cuss. I suppose that means I shoved all my dirt under the rug. I tried to raise all of you that way too. Like some Hindu or Platonist. You know, wealth stinks, material things are for the birds, and so on. I still believe it. All these dollars are like little mirrors. 'Self, self, self,' That's all they say. Or *dough.* Uncooked gunk that sits in your stomach and gives you a bellyache."

"You could give it away."

"I've actually thought of that. But I can't. I'm tight as a

drum. Worse than ever. Thank God, I still have the *Letter,* though it's going quarterly now. You know that, don't you?"

"Of course I do, Dad. I read every issue."

I kissed her cheek. "You're something. Anyway, I've got more free time than I've ever had. That, too, I have to learn to handle. Though I've always been a good idler."

"That's crazy, Dad. You're the least idle person I've ever seen."

"You're wrong, Liv. It's why I've never been able to work for anybody else. So I could sit around and stare at my shoes when I wanted to. I do an awful lot of shoe staring now. I stare, I lounge, I dress, I drink a little wine, I stare some more, then maybe I go through a few editing motions. Occasionally I improvise a cliché. I contemplate my feelings a lot. It's completely self-indulgent. Even telling you is self-indulgent."

"You complicate things so, Dad. I wonder why. Maybe because you've spent so much time clarifying other people's work. Or am I being too complicated?" She tossed up her arms, a lacy windmill. "Let's live it up, today, anyway. What else are these things good for?"

"I know. It's nuts, isn't it. Look, you take off. I'll catch you later. You look just wonderful, and this is a wonderful day." I drew her up and kissed her cheek again—I never kissed children, relatives, or old friends on the mouth—and gave her a small shove toward a group of young laughers surrounding Maria. I took a glass of champagne from a circulating waiter and drank it on the other side of the garden by a lattice of honeysuckle. The beautiful, dense perfume, the small-saw buzz of the insects flying out of the blue flowers, the brilliant heat, the champagne, the presence of most of those I loved most—I let myself open up. Everyone was safe today. There was singing, some soft rock no-sense thing. "Lay down your something and you will see the something you've been something for." I drank more champagne, and felt it turn to sweat. Whew. Too much. I didn't need all this spinning and dazzlement. There were hands on my shoulders. "Dad." I jumped as if the honeysuckle had spoken. It was Jenny. "What're you doing off by yourself?"

"Waiting for you."

Back from her three years in Africa—during which I'd seen her but a week two Christmases ago—Jenny took getting used to. Half of her seemed new. She was tanner, fuller. She'd cut her bright brown hair short. I could see some of mother in her, though Jenny was finer-looking, less harsh-looking, an aristocrat. "I've almost forgotten what you look like." Stepping back a little to take in her dress, a lot of green and gold that looked better-cut, better sewn, than what I remembered of her clothes. She looked prosperous, though as far as I knew, you don't make great fortunes in the diplomatic corps, and Oliver had no family money. "You look great. Expensive."

Jenny has the least expletive of laughs. There's just a store of merriment ready to fall out of her face at a flick of humor or kindness. She's so mild and pleasant, it surprises even those who know her best that she usually gets what she wants. (Though, too, she usually manages to seem satisfied with what she has.) She's the child I feel I know least.

"Not for you," she said.

Her voice, like Emma's, is something wonderful. Exceptionally clear and lyric. (Agnes says that it's not Jenny's eyes but her voice that's the window of her soul.) She and Oliver were back for his two-year Washington assignment, and she hoped to finish her dissertation. She was at the Library of Congress every day. She sent me a postcard of the Reading Room. "Most people don't think of this as their office, but I

do. Look at the far left. The dot in the blue sweater. See?"
Sure enough, it was Jenny. She said being away from a good
library had been the worst thing about Africa.

She took my arm, and we walked out of the sun into the
patio. Across the way, Agnes, in a dress too dark for the
occasion, was listening cheerily to Mrs. Pengratz and her
old mother. The classic Agnes bit of enduring—or supply-
ing—boredom. Her crook's mouth—one side attentive, the
other grim—gave her away.

Jenny brought me a plate of crabmeat— she always knew
other people's likes—and we sat on a puffy lounge. "Some
grand wedding," she said. "Wouldn't Grandpa and
Grandma have loved it? She was so upset I didn't marry
properly." Jenny and Oliver had married quickly before
going to—and partly to simplify the protocol of living in—
Africa.

"Grandpa wouldn't have known what was going on."

"I suppose not. Such a darling man, even when he was
gaga."

"All those years of hacking flesh used up his meanness.
Do you remember that day you and I took him to the Art
Institute?"

"No. Are you sure it was me? Not Jack or Ben?"

"I thought it was you. Grandpa got all Sundayed up in
one of those red four-in-hands my Grandpa Riemer left
him. I don't think he'd ever been in an art museum. He
loved the *Grand Jatte*. He said, 'I didn't know there were
such beautiful things in the world.' "

"That's beautiful."

"How are *you*, Jen-heart?"

"About the same."

But there was something in the lively voice. Something
unsaid. Was it Oliver? Or was it only my double-entry view
of happiness: one's marrying here, so one must be splitting

there. "Sure there's not something you want to talk about?"
"There's always lots to talk about."

Maybe she's pregnant and doesn't want to steal limelight
from Jack and Maria. That would be a wholly different
cake. "You're not—not in a delicate condition, by any
chance?"

"Delicate? Me? It's only your diction that's delicate, Dad.
No, I'm not ready for that yet. I'm not sure I ever will be."

"I'm sorry, sweetheart. Forgive my clumsiness. I guess I
enjoyed you so much the idea of having another version
pushed me where I had no right to go."

"No intrusion. Most of my business is yours. I don't feel
protective about it." Though we both knew she did. "I'm
just afraid of what I'd become if I had children."

"You'd just have another you, Jenny. Or a fascinating
variation of you. Why would you change?"

"I'm afraid of the selfishness of it. Being so absorbed in
the baby, I'd lose everything else. I've seen it in my
friends."

"That's nature. Everything you are is needed. It's not a
bad thing."

"That doesn't make it less narrow. Or mothers less
boring. If people want it, fine, though I think lots of
women want it because they know other people want it for
them. Or through them." I felt a little heat on my face. I
was her "other people." She must have seen it, for she
flushed too. "Which is also fine, maybe right—there have
to *be* children—and if you've been happy with something
you want people you love to be happy the same way." The
rapidity of conciliation was also discomforting. As if Jenny
couldn't bear to have a shadow on our relationship for a
second. Dear, in a way, but sad, for though I treasured our
relationship, it shouldn't be as important as the one that
seemed troubled or the one that she disclaimed. Or was I

misreading her? Maybe Jenny had just absorbed the habits of diplomatic life, the endless ingratiation of other people's sensitivity? The puzzle, though, was the weight of her desire not to be boring or bored. Was it having the mother—and father—she did that made that so important for her? But it couldn't—at least shouldn't—be the reason she didn't want to have a child. Maybe Jenny was—like me—deeply lazy and just couldn't face the drudgery of a child's demands. (As her mother had faced them—and cheerfully—over and over.) So full of brightness, so pretty in the lemony, grassy dress with its expensive tucks, her body so full and strong in it—not solid like Livy's but full in the breasts and hips, a mother's body under the ballerina face with its unworldly intensity, though—as if this sunlight were a microscope—I could see for the first time miniscule zippers of flesh at the edge of her mouth and eyes. Oh, my. "I've said too much, Jen. I want your happiness, any way you want it."

"I know, Dad. I've always believed that. Maybe that's made me selfish."

Maybe it has, I thought, but I could not say that to a much blacker kettle. Nor did I have the right to use her to breed my future. Though no one but one's children could. Maybe that too she knew, and felt it as another assignment, the sort of imposed obligation which already dominated her life.

Like me again, Jenny wanted self-employment. The riches of the Library of Congress were her freedom. There she made her own choices. That she'd narrowed them around her book on the ruinous families of literature only reinforced her opposition to what I and —in my view—her maternal body called for. I should have guessed her book was a declaration of independence.

We sat for a bit without saying anything, a rarity in the

Riemer family (where everything was either loudly up front or loudly concealed). Then Jenny said we should round up a send-off for Jack and Maria, people were taking off for the airport.

I felt a little heavier in every way than when I'd sat down with her.

Retrospection is, at least for me, like one of those Escher illusion etchings which are transformed by your regard: the second look turns depth into shallowness, out into in, the castle into the doghouse, the bird into the giant's eye.

Most of the time, I look back on Jack's wedding as a time of sweetness and recovery. The shadows in Livy and Jenny only deepen and beautify the retrospective light. Now and then, I think of it as farcical or sad, since the marriage lasted scarcely longer than the dogwood blossoms. It's not just the pleasures of the days themselves, but what happened to me after them.

I'd had a lot of bad time that winter. Emma said it was a belated reaction to the deaths of my parents. "Little Orphan Cyrus. Abandoned at fifty." Who knows? (I certainly thought of my parents far more often than when they'd lived.) In any case, I'd spent much of February and March in bed. "I haven't taken to my bed," I told Emma. "It's taken to me." It had started with a cold. I hadn't gone to bed with a cold for decades, yet in February I turned into the little boy my mother had pampered with tea and honey. Now Emma was mother. She brought me meals on trays, got me books from the library, administered pills and helped me steam my sinuses. Nights, she crawled in with me to watch the serial programs whose mindless glamor gripped us week to week. (We could hardly wait to find out who had cheated, exposed, shot, or divorced whom in the baronies of Denver and Dallas.) When my nose, chest, and throat finally cleared, I stayed in bed anyway, editing copy, answering mail, writing checks, calling contributors. Often I didn't get up till two or three o'clock, and then only to walk down the hall to my office or occasionally out to the bank. I was in bed so much I sometimes thought I wasn't. The bed was desk, chair, even plane and train, for I drifted off on every sort of expedition. Emma said, "My little one needs adventure. Needs need."

But I didn't. Life streamed in and out of bed; and time as well: it had never passed so quickly. In the *Sun-Times* I read an article about Hugh Hefner. He'd spent years in bed editing his magazines and bringing playmates and the other good things of the world there. An inverted Magellan. There were far more gifted cavaliers of the sack: Descartes, Proust, Churchill, Keynes, Picasso. All worked horizontal wonders while the world's time punchers went their vertical way.

Propped on pillows, turkey sandwich and peppermint herbal tea beside me on the table, Beethoven sonatas and Bach chaconnes coming in on WFMT, I went over articles on Tourette's Syndrome and nuclear catastrophe. (I loved doing disaster pieces.) While I chewed chicken salad, I red-penciled sentences about humanoid survivors in dead land-scapes.

The day I returned from the wedding, I went over to Emma's place. Bare feet on her Moroccan hassock—bought from a Spiegel catalog—spooning rum raisin ice cream out of a Haagen Dasz carton, she was watching an afternoon talk show. Once again she was between jobs. I changed into the house pants I keep *chez elle*—orange-and-red-striped, a circus affair I'd bought for eight bucks on Maxwell Street after buying Ben a basketball at Kelly's—and sat next to her. The host—strange word, out of *hostis*, "stranger," so "guest"—was a fellow with wavy gray hair and a shark's smile, which did not conceal stupidity. He was asking a beautiful actress about her films, love life, ambitions, fears. Every question interrupted an answer. The actress tried wit, obliquity. Nothing was witty or oblique enough. She tried gestures, touched his arm; he asked was she coming on with him. Finally, she retreated to the last ditch of celebrities and crooks, the *bocca chiusa*, silence.

Said Emma, "Her looks are throwing him for a loop. He can't handle it."

Beauty, I thought, it's like those winds they give names to—sirocco, mistral, harmattan, chinook, sukavei—they change wherever they blow, lives and laws are arranged around them. (Murder someone during the mistral, and you got a lighter sentence.) Even in this last part of the twentieth century, when millions transformed themselves into beauties—and a walk down a great avenue shows more of them than a French king would have seen in years—a beauty deforms the space and time around her. I was still full of wedding beauty. Emma saw my excitement. I tried to play it down. "Yes, it went well. Thank God I only had to pay for the one dinner. Bad enough. It cost me a thousand bucks. Still, as those anachronisms go, it was a good show."

"And now," Emma said, with the tranquillity I knew was the surface of almost any other feeling, "Maria's more legitimate than me."

"Baloney."

"Not baloney. She's Mrs. Riemer."

"As a matter of fact, I think she kept her maiden name."

"Doesn't matter. The Riemersphere has another official planet. And Kong's outside, all by himself, holding onto the universe for dear life. Go look at the wall. There's a new slogan."

I went ino a bedroom and looked up and down the besilvered crimson heart. "I don't see it. Where is it?"

"A foot left of the bed lamp. In the Kong section. Under 'KONG IS REAL' "

There it was in her beautiful silvery script, "KONG WON'T LET GO," and, beside it, an unusual dividend, a shivery sketch of a hairy silver arm clutching the Empire State Building, while the other was raised in the black power salute.

"It's a great one, sweeetie. But Kong's in no danger."

"How do you know?"

"What does that mean? Who knows better?"

"Not you," said Emma. "You'd let me fall and not even know you had."

"I don't get it."

"You just did by going to the wedding without me."

"I thought we agreed it wasn't the right time to—"

"It never is. But you don't know what I feel. You don't even know what you feel. Even Livy says you're less in touch with your unconscious than anyone she knows."

"What!" That shook me, not the observation, which seemed screwy to me, but the fact of Emma and Livy discussing me. I didn't mind them indicting me to my face, I could handle that. But behind-the-back analysis upset me. The children spent half their lives analyzing those closest to them. They were like little Bloomsburyites, dishing sublime dirt. (But Keynes and Strachey, Woolf and the Stephens girls, were knocking down mountains of Victorian restraint. Who'd restrained my kids?) The human mouth is the true Pandora's box. "I don't think Livy believes half the crap that comes out of her mouth. I don't believe much in knowing myself, but if I knew myself as little as I think they know me, I'd be in trouble. God knows I don't want

Chinese ancestor worship from them. I don't want to be a daguerreotype in one of my grandfather's frock coats—but all this demystifying analysis won't grow beans."

"Wrong tradition," said Emma. "You're right out of your own Old Testament: what counts can't be understood, shouldn't be talked about. 'God is great, exceeding our knowledge.' The first chauvinist. Pure Riemer."

"Well, if you mean I'm not a little Bloomsburyite, interested in the origin of every spot of semen, you bet. As far as I'm concerned, analysis destroys relationships." The more my children analyzed each other, the more interdependent they grew. That seemed to be their idea of family. (Though they're far closer to me than I was to my parents. In that household we didn't analyze, only reacted to each other. Of course, I didn't have any siblings. And despite the cleavers, carcasses, bloodied chops, and briskets which paid our rent, life there was virtuous and temperate.) "As for analyzing deity, that's for the birds. I don't care if it's Einstein or Saint Paul, any lousy little human being who pretends his miserable brain has one inkling of one iota of one breath of any understanding whatsoever of what's really going on in this universe ought to be strung up."

"I know," said Emma. "And crucified. You guys did that once."

The actress leaned away from a grinning barb. I made out the outline of her breasts in the loose sweater. She was really extraordinary. "I'd like to kill that bastard. Host, from hostile."

"You like her more than me," said Emma, but with her comic doggy pout.

"I like no one more than you."

Home, I went right to my office. A stack of galleys waited on the pew. My deadline these days was leisurely; I hadn't looked at them for a week. I picked up the top galley. "Circadian Dyschronism During Transmeridian Flight." No, I couldn't do it. Often now something happened in my head when I started to work: it felt as if an iron shutter rolled down the middle of the brain. I looked out the window at the horse chestnut tree in my neighbor's yard. A squirrel hurled itself at the trunk and powered into the foliage. I looked at my literature wall: Balzac, Dickens, Plutarch, the Goncourt Journals, Proust. There was a narrow space for the book I'd read on the plane, Mauriac's *Viper's Tangle*. (The tangle was the old lawyer's heart, furious at his hypocritical, cringing children.) A breeze came through the screen. There were tiny clicks from the chestnut tree, vines shimmied on the brick wall. Thackeray. Thucydides. Tolstoy, my time-mate, born like me in August, but in eighteen, not nineteen twenty-eight. Part of my armature of dates. (My father was born in 1887, mother in 1897, Grandpa Riemer born in the year of the California Gold Rush.) What Tolstoy did in 1850, 1860, 1870, I compared to what I did in 1950, 1960, 1970. I'd married earlier, had children earlier. When Tolstoy was soldiering, I worked for the City News Bureau. Tolstoy published *Childhood* in 1852; I put out the first *News Letter* in 1952. (Agnes was also a published writer in 1952: *Austin, the Anteater.*) In 1855 Tolstoy published *Sebastopol Sketches* and was famous. From then on, our careers diverged. I picked up *War and Peace*. Prince Andrew feels he's finished. He visits the Rostovs in the country. At night he overhears Natasha telling Sonia it's so beautiful she'd like to fly out the window. Riding away the next day, he sees an oak tree in bloom. Joy grips him. Life isn't over.

A wedding is also a parent's graduation. I was free, white, pretty rich, and though two and a half times twenty-one, energetic. What Natasha and the oak tree did for Prince Andrew, Robin Tuck and the dogwood did for me. I took out the files of the *News-Letter* and started reading them. What a surprise. How much there was. I was thrilled. Even the editorials seemed fresh. A few were clairvoyant, and most were not badly written. In my head was what I'd said to Robin about making an anthology of them. Why not?

In the busiest, happiest week I'd had in months, I picked out forty of the best pieces, edited out repetitiousness, annotated obscurities, and arranged them into a meaningful sequence. I took a week to write a short preface about the *News-Letter*—"a bridge between the laboratory and the street"—and typed out a title page:

OFF MY CHEST
Selected Commentary from the *Riemer News-Letter*

by
Cyrus Riemer

Even when I typed out this page, I wasn't *really* (tricky word) thinking (another tricky one) of publication, but Emma spotted the secret want and *persuaded* me to send the manuscript to publishers.

During the next six months, half a dozen university presses rejected it more or less summarily, even after I enclosed a letter of recommendation which I'd solicited—on Emma's prompting—from Mel Sorgmund.

Publication I owed to Maria. One day she said she'd heard of a small university press that had just received money to defray the costs of good, but otherwise unprofitable, books. "I've got to see a friend who works there tomorrow," she said. "Why don't I take him your book?"

"Very kind of you, honey, but it's a waste of time." I'd gotten to care for this daughter-in-law, seen the earnest sweetness within the fluent pushiness; I ignored the humorlessness and treasured the sweetness and wit which masked it. Maria was like her face, girlishly charming below the eyes, massive, almost menacing, above. I paid attention to the lower half and let the upper half go its own way. (It went my way.)

A few days later, she called to say her friend had just called to say that the Publication Board had accepted the book.

"Oh, Maria, what a miracle. What a darling you are."

"He says it'll be a few months before it comes out. And you shouldn't expect it to make much of a splash."

"Sweetheart, it's already a splash. I'm practically drowning. I don't need any more than this."

Just as well. The only review of *Off My Chest* was in *Library News:* thirty-five neutral words of description. As for sales, they were strictly personal. Maria and Emma went into Chicago bookstores asking for it. None had copies; a few were persuaded to order it. Maria bought twenty-five copies, Emma—with my money—fifty. Even copies I gave away—to *News-Letter* contributors, friends, and the children—were seldom acknowledged. Livy telephoned congratulations, and Jenny telegraphed that the book was "wonderful, even better than I expected." Ben wrote a long letter of analysis, its only serious review. Serious, though off the wall. He said that my mind, "your *integer vitae*," was "essentially segmental." "I guess that's what it means to be a man of parts, Dad. Of course," he went on, "it's not a bad thing to string pearls together, especially when you're the oyster. It's got something to do with you being a just and patient editor. (It's clear you had an ideal fetal ambience.)

Grandpa Riemer was a middleman between the slaughter-house and the kitchen. In a way so are you: the editorial pencil is your cleaver."

Not the kind of review you'll see in the *New York Times*. (Unless Ben becomes editor.)

Jack said, "It's a beautiful book, Dad. I love the Dürer on the cover. Maria really came through, didn't she?"

"She sure did. I can never thank her enough."

"Well, why shouldn't that dirty money go to a good cause?"

An internal drum roll started up. "What do you mean, Jack? What dirty money?"

"Her dad's. I told you she'd do good things with it. She worked like hell. She's a real American. Making, moving, dealing, getting into the papers. Like her old man. A solvent American thinks he's Alexander the Great. Whether it's steel, pornography, computers, or self-improvement. That's half of commerce now: Becoming What You're Not. Making It. Learning It. Your book fits right in. She still worked like hell for it. These little institutions are loaded with committees. It had to go to this one, that one, then the dean, then the Publication Board. Finally, she wrote the damn president of the university and told him the money was getting restless, and if they wanted it for their profes-sors' books on the ethics of the void, they'd better get off the pot on your book."

"So that's how it was?"

"Sure. At least they got a pretty fair book. I mean you can actually read your sentences and not vomit. And it doesn't pretend to be the *Critique of Pure Reason*."

"No," I said. "It has that in its favor."

I told Emma what Jack said. "I wouldn't have dared use my own money to publish it. So it's turned out I used Robusto's."

"You just said it had to go through all those deans and boards. They wouldn't publish something if they didn't believe in it. That's the point. It's a good book. *That's* the point. But Jack's a shit for telling you."

"That's what I get for raising him to tell the truth."

Emma reached into her years of course work and came up with a mess of authors who'd paid for their own books: Whitman, Proust, Pound, Jane Austen. "And Joyce, Frost, Hemingway—they all had publishing blues, they all needed special help. Lots of them even reviewed their own books under pseudonyms. The main thing is, you have a beautiful book."

And sure enough, that was the feeling that lasted. After all these years, there was *a thing* that was mine. And not just an ordinary thing, but one which contained the best of what I'd done. Print, binding, a designed jacket—Dürer's Saint Anthony lost in his book while, at his feet, a lion gazes off the page. A real thing. Part of culture, listed in *Forthcoming Books,* then *Books in Print,* and—before long—*Books out of Print.* Even this sequence moved me.

IV

For years Agnes had told the children that she wanted "to do one more thing in my life." She applied for the Peace Corps and, after a year of interviews and medical examinations, was accepted. I didn't much look forward to being the children's home base, but for Agnes I was happy. Her intrepidity even became a sort of medal for me. "Ag's going to Rwanda," I told Seldon.

"Ag? Rwanda?"

"My ex-wife's going to teach English and Library Science in East Africa. For the Peace Corps. Fifty-four years old, and she's packing up part and parcel."

"I thought it was your daughter who did that spade work." Seldon had double-faulted away the first set, then slammed two forehands over a fence into Fifty-fifth Street; we quit because we were down to one ball, and went to the Plaka for juice and muffins.

I ignored the small nastiness. "It does seem that Riemers like to work in the ancestral continent of our fellow Chicagoans. Still, Ag is no chicken. I admire her."

"Mish Lillyam wash"—Dochel's mouth was full of juice-soaked muffin—"about a hundred when she went off shome-where. Teaching Punjabis how to eat grits and wipe their asses."

"She was terrific too. Said she'd had to suppress her anguish about blacks for years. India gave her an outlet for her feelings."

"It's real nice of the world to provide outlets for you stifled do-gooders. How about you? You can start up tennis tournaments for Decrepit Colonials. I'm sure you'll find a few you can bamboozle with your effing junk."

"I don't have the guts to do anything. It's all talk with me."

After Livy told me that Agnes had been accepted and had two months to rent her apartment, find her replacement at the library, get her shots and passport, buy clothes, work out her finances, read the pamphlets and books sent from Washington, and psych herself up, not for the idea but the real thing, my head was full of images of her sleeping in a thatched hut under the stars, rattling along stony roads in ancient buses, fetching water in calabashes from village pumps. I was peculiarly excited by all this. For her. Against her. For myself. Against myself. I thought she'd be terrific at it. She'd been at the nurturing and instructing business her whole adult life. It was her profession, her disposition, her gift. The Peace Corps was made for her: American benevolence bringing its optimistic message to the wilder-ness. The Peace Corps was Camelot's legacy: its knights went into the world, did their good deeds, and returned to the Round Table with adventures and conversions. It was summer camp, boy-and-girl scouts, evangelism, one-worldism, everything the country needed to cover the muscles of its trade and bellicosity. What better missionary than Agnes Lozzicki Riemer? When Livy told me that she'd first been rejected for medical reasons, I felt terrible for her. "She's got an enlarged heart," said Livy.

"How appropriate."

"The doctor says a slight spinal curvature creates a cavity the heart fills."

"She's had it all her life and worked like a dog with it. I don't see why that should hold her back. She should get a second opinion."

Which is what happened, and when I heard the second opinion was positive, I was delighted, though I would miss running into her on the street, miss our Christmas reunions. (I would not miss the reminder of our failure, the small strains like ice bits in an April stream.) There was also relief about Agnes's future. I was always afraid she'd get sick and couldn't work. She had next to no money, and her pension was miserable. Somehow or other, I'd have to take care of her. The arrangement with the Peace Corps was ideal: after her African assignment, she'd be given one in the States and she'd have a federal pension. The assignment, though, wouldn't be in Chicago.

Our family life was essentially over: except for a wedding, it was unlikely that all the Riemers would ever be in the same town again.

Leaving, Agnes revealed how much space she'd occupied. She was feted by colleagues, friends, the parents of children in her library programs. There were letters, presents, cards, poems, parties with speeches, presentations of plaques, watches, books about Africa, luggage, first-aid packets, Bibles. The mother of a retarded boy she had taught to read gave her a medallion she'd received from her mother. When

Agnes tried to refuse it, she said it would only have meaning for her if Agnes accepted it and later passed it on to "some other precious person."

These farewells drained her. Then a winter cold hung on and carved pounds off her. I'd never seen her look so small. She was five-five, but the sixty-five inches seemed to double back on each other. She weighed about ninety pounds and walked as if she were at the bottom of the sea. She'd never been a quick mover, but now, in the last days, she packed and repacked her bags, clinging to the detailed instruction booklet as a despairing communicant clings to the letters and commas of his scripture—the only ladder out of the depths. She piled the presents and the letters she intended to answer, wrote out the final checks to the gas and electric companies, assembled documents and clothes in storage boxes, and talked out money and apartment matters with Livy, who was to handle them. The slugworm pace of all this looked to me like her way of delaying the excitement she'd chosen for herself, a way of preventing anxiety from taking the rest of the meat off her bones.

To my surprise, I was plenty anxious myself. I feared for Agnes, thin good person whom I'd wronged and been wronged by, whom I'd loved and, in a scarcely noticed part of myself, apparently still loved. (Was—in a way—still true to and about. I wanted to hear nothing against her, and remembered nothing of the many bad times we'd had.)

The children came to Chicago to say good-bye to her. "The last Riemer hurrah," said Livy.

The in-laws couldn't make it: Oliver couldn't get leave and Maria was off "seeing," said Jack, "what Robusto money could squeeze out of the world, ugh."

I missed Maria, and it was much more than gratitude for the book. We'd never figured out what she should call me. I

invited, and she'd tried out, "Dad," but she had her own
dad, and, as Jack said, he was "dad enough for anyone."
"Mister" was impossible, and neither of us felt comfortable
with "Cy." The absence of an easy vocative was a leak in our
boat. Still, we'd found a way of talking to and enjoying each
other. I also felt she was Jack's lifeline; at least his bridle. It
had been months since he'd left Moshur and Dochel for New
York, and, as far as I could see, he did nothing there. His
old profession. "I was looking forward to seeing her, Jack.
The only time I see her now is on television."

"You and me both."

I thought that was persiflage. "She seems to be one of
TV's favorite guests."

"She's a great guest," said Jack.

I still suspected nothing. I was preoccupied with the
other loss, the last act of what Emma called "the Riemer
Follies."

I spent every evening of Agnes's last Chicago week at her
apartment. I hadn't spent so much time with her since I'd
left the house a dozen years ago. It felt both strange and
natural to be back as an intimate of the house, to see Agnes
in her bathrobe, the small-boned, aging woman whom her
clothed, made-up, energetic day-self covered up. I'd never
seen her in such bad shape, blue trenches of fatigue under
her eyes, crimson blotches in her cheeks. So much of her had
been spent.

A couple of nights before she took off, I found her alone.
"Jenny and Jack are walking Verg," she said. Down the hall
I could hear the television going. It was Ben and Nancy
Triplett—who was to be the newest Riemer—wrapped in
each other in front of it. (It didn't matter what programs. It
was their sonic Chinese Wall.) "What's wrong, Agnes?"

"I don't know. Something I can't handle."

"Of course. It's a terribly anxious time for you."

I followed her into the living room and sat in the black leather chair I'd bought a quarter of a century ago for my family throne. It was the one good chair bought in our twenty years together. She lay on the couch, something I couldn't remember her doing in front of me in all these years of divorce. (The couch had come to us from my parents after they'd moved from Amsterdam Avenue to the East Side. Agnes had had its gold pillows recovered in a mind-boggling pattern: a hundred peg-legged Ahabs exchanging smiles with a hundred white whales.)

"I've never felt like this," she said. "I hate not being able to do anything about it."

The end of the day hung by the window in golden dust. The upper part of Agnes's head was in shadow, but the dust lit that odd two-tiered crook's mouth of hers, sensuous and cynical at once, as if it both offered itself and mocked the offering. Isolated in the light, it seemed to say something which had nothing to do with what came out of it, a sort of physiological subtext that I read as, "Why have you never understood?"

The television set intruded the news: a paraplegic arrested for molesting his six-year-old niece.

"In a couple of days it'll all be over, Ag. Once you're in the air, you'll be fine. I think you've been terrific. If I'd had to do a tenth of what you've done, I'd be in a hospital. I don't sleep for a week before a plane to New York."

"I didn't know that. What's it like?"

"Nausea, headaches, heart doing a rhumba, heaviness behind the eyes, general anxiety."

"I've been thinking it's just me, that there's something wrong with me and I won't make it. I've burned the bridges, job, apartment, everything."

How nice it was talking with her this way. It was as if we

were reaching back for some of what we'd emotionally and legally abandoned. Two nights before, she'd asked the children to bunch for a picture, then said, "You too, Cy." She wanted me in the family picture she'd show around the African hills. I guess in both of us strong feelings were breaking down the structures which had been built to resist them.

It was getting darker in the room. As I strained to see her, it really came to me that she wouldn't be around, that from now on I would be *home*. My apartment, big enough only for me—and for Emma's complaints about it—would be where visiting children would stay. It would be loud with their awful music and the noise of large bodies clumping around. They'd be in the toilets and bathtubs when I wanted to use them. All the ad-lib habits of solitude, which Emma took in stride and made light of, would be censored: I wouldn't be able to walk around naked, would have to set a good example, make the bed, wash the dishes, pick things off the floor. I was not only a father, I'd have to be—as I used to be—the example of fathering. When they were little, we had an easy, if passionate, sometimes riotous and obscene family life, but that was when the family was the only show in our lives. Since then, silence and solitude had become my family. The private self, which in those days had hidden out, was now almost everything. Only Emma knew how to accommodate it.

The door opened. In came Vergil on the confident plick-plick of his nails and the haughty jingle of his leash. Jack and Jenny followed him. "Hi, Dad," they said. But there was a waver in their voices, and when they came closer, they seemed discomforted. I suppose they hadn't expected me so early, perhaps they'd been talking about me. I kissed Jenny and patted Jack on the shoulder. He wore a T-shirt streaked in front with bright colors. He also wore—what he'd worn indoors and out all week—a white baseball cap with a green bill on which was inscribed *Riverside Drivers.*

Agnes had sat up. "Dad's been helping me. It turns out he has travel anxiety too. It makes me feel normal."

"Don't go that far," said Jack. He sat beside and put his arm around her. She looked half his size.

Jenny said, "We'd better finish packing, Mom. I'll do it if you want me to."

"No, I'll come with you." She followed Jenny down the hall. I called after her, "Could you get Ben and Nancy to lower that television, please, Ag? I'd like to talk to Jack in peace."

The day she'd come to Chicago Jenny had taken me aside and said she thought Jack was having a rough time. "I think we should try to give him a boost."

"How so, Jen? Are you sure it isn't something a job couldn't smooth out?"

"He hears enough of that from Maria, Dad. From us he needs support."

Now I said, "I hear things are a little rough, Jack."

"Things are fine," he said.

"A few rough spots with Maria?"

"A few. Nothing I can't hop over."

"She a good hopper too?"

"Not bad. Not as good as me though. I have an easier nature than you guys."

"You're lucky."

"I am," he said. "And it's so great to be back in New York. There's a novel in every face. Every other table's a dinner with André." This was his latest favorite movie.

"Permanent world's fair, eh?"

"There isn't enough time to see a billionth of it."

This enthusiasm annoyed me. Here Agnes was putting her whole life up for grabs, while this thirty-year-old man in a boy's baseball cap proclaimed the infinite riches in his little room. Never had he seemed so beside the point to me. Still, I had promised Jenny to boost, not knock. "The grail in every ash can, eh?"

"That's it."

"If only it were the eighteenth century, even the nineteenth, and you were the son of a duke, your self-satisfaction would be socially acceptable. No one would expect any more of you, and you wouldn't have to feel—what I'm sure you do—shame."

"I feel less shame than you think. I told you I'm a more lighthearted guy than you are. I don't need to be a duke. That's the point. I've learned to be happy with very little."

"How about making someone else happy?"

"Emotionally I'm for laissez-faire. Not that I want to make people unhappy."

I started to say that's just what he did, his mother, me, and apparently Maria, if no one else. Instead I said, "You're a gifted person, Jack. You're smart, energetic, you know a lot, you're sweet and generous. What I'm scared of is that you won't use your gifts, and they'll rust away. I mean if life is only a long buffet table—"

"You know it isn't that for me."

"Well, what is—"

"I've got so many things to work out, I'd need fifty lives. Even Wittgenstein couldn't solve all the things I want to. I don't talk about things because I haven't done them yet. I've got a hundred plans. I'd like to dig out the premises of lives which appear not to have any. You know, like Keynes said, every so-called practical man's the prisoner of some outmoded economist. I know you are uncomfortable with bums, street people; I'm not. I get along with everybody. I think I could do for them what Ved Mehta did for the Oxford philosophers and the historians. I'd call the book *Sinkers*. Because sinking's really a form of swimming."

"Well, this is more like it, Jack. It's a grand idea. Maybe if you could get some of it on paper, you could get a grant. Meanwhile, you could get a—"

"Maybes and ifs." He laced his hands behind his head and threw his legs under the coffee table.

"Once you concentrate on something, I know you can bring it off. Just a page a day. In a year, you'd have three hundred sixty-five pages."

"I concentrate plenty on Pac-Man and still can't lick it." He was just not going to play in my key. If his life meant anything, it meant that. "See, my trouble is, I've spent years—ever since I was fifteen, no, ten—thinking up ways to make my life pleasant. When it comes to *not* concentrating, I'm a real virtuoso."

Christ Almighty. Such confusion and such phoniness. All that Riemer flesh busting out of a boy's T-shirt, ragged jeans, ratty sneakers, absurd cap. Ludicrous, infuriating, heartbreaking. I said, "I'm afraid for you." I know I saw a flick of joy in his face.

"That's silly. I know how to take care of myself."

"I see that too. I also see you're able to endure a life most fellows raised like you couldn't. I guess that's admirable. I mean you don't just endure, you make the best of it. You might even be able to make it in prison."

To my surprise, something like a genuine groan came out of him. He started rocking back and forth, then put his head down into his palms. The baseball cap tipped over his ear and landed mouth up on the floor. "Jack, I don't mean you'll end up in prison. Though I have waked up at night scared you'd do something, maybe for a friend, I don't know, you'd step over the line, and before you knew where you were . . . boom. I've also been scared you'd get sick and have to settle for tenth-rate care."

"Or that you'd have to pay for it."

"Yes, maybe, since my insurance hasn't covered you for years. Is that so foolish? That you could break us all, mom, Jenny, all of us."

"I take care of myself. I don't ask for anything."

"But I don't know how you do it now. Maria's gone off. How do you live? Day by day, I mean?"

"That's my business."

"Right. It's all your business, though none of it looks very busy."

"Go on. Pile it on."

"I don't want to pile it on."

"Somehow you always do."

"I guess I do. Years ago you told me I gave you too much advice. And not enough money."

"I don't ask you for money."

"Children don't need to ask. I know I've used it to discipline you."

"Why not say *punish?* Punishment pleases the punisher."

"Sure, that was there too, I'm sure. Though I didn't feel it that way."

There was no way of penetrating. Maybe embrace, but that was impossible. It was too late for that. (Damn the manacles this idler put on so much. Troublemakers use up so much of the world.) I said, " 'The sluggard's wiser in his own conceit, than seven men who can render or reason.' That's another text for you."

"Proverbs. You sent me 'The slothful man says, there's a

lion in the way.' And I read the rest of them. I told you then
I knew I used everything as a lion. Don't you think I know
I'm my own biggest lion?"

"Okay, then, if you know it, it's terrific. Just take the
next step."

"What? Go to jail?"

"You won't let me say anything right. You just dodge
and dodge. You have to make me the villain." His head
shook negatives over the couch. In its boy's smallness, I saw
the bare patch the baseball cap was meant to cover. Back
and forth, he shook it. Shutting out what he didn't want to
hear? Putting on a show? I never knew with him. "Why not
talk to someone who can help you straighten out? It would
be a gift to me to let me pay for it. My God, you've got so
much, and all I can see is it spilling out of you. And you
watching it spill. You can't keep going on day by day
amusing yourself. In fact, you know you're not amusing
yourself. That's why you drink any time you can find a
bottle and smoke your dope, and go to every movie and read
every book—as long as they'll let you stand in the bookstore—and drown yourself in the tube."

"What's wrong with having a good time?"

"I want to say, 'Plenty. In your case.' Because every good
time you have's a rebuke to the deeper you, the you I've put
in you, the you that's me. Good or bad, it's there and been
there from the beginning. I've got it just as crazily as you
do, and it's driven me the way you're driven by it."

He scooped up the cap and put it back on. I guess it
meant he was back in uniform, ready to play his game
again. "I don't think so. We're totally different. I make my
own pace."

I said I was glad but my feelings doubled over themselves, which Jack knew as well as I. He would always

manage to find the knife in what I said. (Was it because the knife was always there?) He'd said things had started when he was ten. Where had I been then? Half in, half out, of the house, meeting my X's and Y's, the lies heavy in my face, the lies I needed, I thought, to protect him and the others. Had Jack inhaled that duplicity? No, it was Livy who was ten, Jack was seventeen or eighteen. Neither he nor I could use that as his excuse.

The next morning, as I concentrated on the day's first decisions—the choice of eggs or granola, toast or muffins—the phone rang. At such an hour, the ring is a menace; either an emergency or a wrong number. Jenny. "Sorry to call so early, Dad, I know you don't like it. But I want to see you. Can I run over for a few minutes?"

"Is anything wrong?"

"Just want to talk."

I don't like morning talks, especially early ones. (My preferred morning vocabulary is "Deuce" and "Fault.") Still, it was almost always a joy to see Jenny. "See you soon."

Sooner than I'd thought. She must have actually run. The speaker emitted its sonorous honk as I was pouring dark African tea—last of a packet I'd bought a year ago at the now-gone Stop-n-Shop—through the strainer's mesh. It spilled and made a grainy lake on the white counter. "Scheiss." A poor beginning.

"Hi, Dad."

There was something wrong in her face, an exceptional heightening of her fine color. It made me refrain from the usual hug and kiss. "Hi, Jen, what's up?"

There was to be no interval of small talk. She began in the hall on the way back to the kitchen. "Dad, how could you talk to Jack the way you did after what I'd said?"

"What do you mean?"

"You said you wouldn't get after him, you'd only say good things to him."

No wonder invasions counted on surprise. I managed to fill a mug and then answered. "But that's what I did. Or tried to do. Do you want tea?"

An angry headshake. "If you did, it just shows how unconsciously destructive you are. Of those you love. How you can't stand equality in the people around you."

"I don't get this, Jen. You mean Mel Sorgmund?"

"No. You can stand to have people above you, or below you, just not equal. Not Jack, not me, certainly not mom. And that's the way it is with Emma. You found your companion in someone who'll heap praise on you, kowtow and *sheiko* and wash you with adoration."

"I don't agree with you. I don't think it's true. And why you're saying it, I don't know. Let's go inside." We went down the long hall, and I sat in the bentwood rocker. Jenny was clearly tempted to stand—the accusatory stance—but, despite her anger, she sat. I said, "It sounds as if you're expressing feelings you've held in for a long time."

"Oh, I am. Since I've been a little girl. I've seen how you bullied Jack, told him how bad his work was, how he should do this and not that, how you corrected and corrected him, following him around the house, yelling. And I know you write him little cards quoting the Bible and God knows what else, telling him how lazy he is, knocking him every way you can think of. *It's awful.*" Her face was bright with anger, her veins bulged bluely in her strong throat. The least critical of the children, she'd hardly ever said even an indirect word of criticism to me. Now it was as if her mildness had turned inside out, as if she'd made up her mind to flush out every fear, including that of breaking the filial decorum which counted so much for both of us. (It did not substitute for, only channeled affection.) It was clear to me that she was saying what she felt had—*at last*—to be said. And what I felt was not a revelation about myself, but something more shaking, the revelation of what this loving daughter had felt about—and concealed from—me. Oh, I'd seen some of it in her book, in the insights into King Lear and other dominating fathers (including that—to me— almost meaningless swarm of verbal paternity, Humphrey Chimpden Earwicker), but that was indirect. It had surprised, even disturbed me, but it was different. That this generous, respectful, loving, quietly able person was also a powerful critical intelligence, able to formulate insights which drew on analysis of her own feelings as well as texts, was one thing; this was another.

What to do? Interrupt? Challenge? Correct (what I was sure was untruth)? Express my own outrage at the expression of hers? I felt anger and the organizing energy of argument. (Not, though—to my relief—hatred.) "All right, Jen, I have been hard on him, but only after I've seen what I've seen, my own son throwing away his life and boasting about it. That's what I call destructiveness. All right, I'm part of a terrible—maybe *the* terrible, if your book and Ben's too are right—human tradition. The tyrant father taking out his own furies on his children's bodies and souls. All right, I can recognize some truth there, but I know, not just believe, I know it's not the whole story."

"Of course it's not. I know that too, Dad." Thank God, a small turn. "You can be terrifically generous—"

"You don't have to take back, you don't have to soft-soap—"

"I'm not. I'm just trying to say everything. Especially what I've never said, the destructiveness that's there with the generosity and love. It's hurt Jack—"

"Has it hurt you?"

"Probably, I don't know. You've always been easier on me. I think it's hurt you most of all." I started to say, "At least it's hurting me now," but didn't. "You tell us how you've been sliding, how you feel you've not done what you could have done—"

"I don't think this is what you came to say, Jenny."

"Though you pulled yourself up and wrote—"

"Pulled myself down."

"Don't top me, Dad. You pulled yourself together and wrote *Off My Chest*. But suppose Jack wrote a better book, he's got the talent for it. *I think you'd cut him down.* I think you don't want him to rival you."

"Oh, Christ, Jen, not even Ann Landers gets away with this. This isn't even good enough for fortune cookies anymore." No wonder Lear threw Cordelia out of England.

"It doesn't mean it isn't true."

"It's just too easy and gross to say."

"It isn't too easy." Her face was bright as blood now. "I've never said it."

"Accusing's easy."

"You should know that."

"Accusing's easy when you accuse some people. But Jack's a duck's back. Accuse Saint Francis of avarice, he'd find an avaricious corner in his heart, or Mother Theresa a lecherous one. I don't mean Jack isn't a great admitter of faults, he just makes admission a game. Cards on the table, calling spades spades, getting to the bottom line, oh, it's great sport. Letting your hair down, what could be better? It's so modern, so profound, getting at the truth within the truth, like hunting for ultimate particles. Atoms, nuclei, positrons, mesons, quarks, on and on until there's nothing but the steam of conception. And that's the point. Make an

intellectual or even an emotional game of it and you don't
have to do anything about it."

"But that's my point," she said. "That's what you do.
You conceptualize your feelings out of existence. You say
you love Jack, but what do you do for him?"

"Jenny, I swear—maybe I've got no right to swear, but I
think, I think deeply that I want Jack to have a great life.
Whenever he does something good, I feel a kind of ecstasy."

"Sure, when he's making money or wearing a necktie
every day." Her eyebrows were raised, little skeptic arches
on that long, subtly colored face, with its breathy lips, the
Degas ballerina coming offstage half in and half out of the
performance lights. The eyebrows were offstage, critical,
like one tier of her mother's mouth.

"Jenny, I want Jack—I want all of you, all kids—to have
as much, *to be* as much as possible. It breaks my heart, all
right, maybe half my heart, that Jack has so little. Is so
little. And now, it seems, he's even lost Maria."

"That's no loss."

"I disagree." My heart was rumbling. I squeezed the flat
side of my hexagonal mug. The resistance of odd space in
my grip. And, between Jenny and me, an odd space; a
resistance. That part of me which wanted the affable,
spoofing, even critical affection of my children, had been
shown the door. I sipped the black tea, five times the
strength of the tea-bagged water I often drank. (Once I'd
forgotten to drop a bag into the hot water and had drunk it,
thinking it only exceptionally weak tea, till Emma pointed
to the unused bag by the saucer.) The tea bit my tongue,
and I spat it back, missing the mug, wetting my orange-
and-blood-striped housepants near the loose zipper. I
shouldn't wear them when my daughters come, or, for that
matter, my sons.

"Is something wrong? Here, I'll get a cloth."

"No, nothing. You're just shaking me up. Look, Jenny, I did try last night with Jack. I had in mind what you said. I praised his ability to endure."

"But not his tal——"

"Let me finish. Christ."

Flush, respect. "Sorry."

"His talent too. I said—I've written him—doesn't he show you those letters? I wrote I thought he could do anything if he wanted."

"He knew what you really felt."

I felt myself rising around my feelings, though knowing—in this exceptionally self-conscious moment—that the rise might be a cover, as everything I'd said might be a cover, for the ancient hatred in the inner brain, man wolf to man. (Or worse, as studies of these good social creatures showed.) "If you think it gratifies me to have Jack living off Maria or Jacqueline or Sondra or whoever he's living off now, if you think I like it that he doesn't have money for stamps or beer or that he has so little he has to advertise the littleness as his only possession and has to deprecate whatever good things he *has* done to maintain the purity of his nothingness, if you think that brings me pleasure, you're either crazy or it must be true at so deep a level that it's never once touched my consciousness. *I want him to be what he can be proud of.*"

"Part of you wants it."

"All right, part of me wants it. And another part of me is a great twinge of love, pity, dismay, and hope begging for him to have it."

"Then why don't you help him? You have money now. You give it to me, to Ben, to Livy, not to Jack. Not for years."

143

"When he was growing up, I didn't have it for him. Or for you. It took every nickel—and plenty of nickels from my parents—to get you through college."

"I know that. But now why? Withholding money is withholding love."

"Because he admits, sometimes he boasts of being a moocher—which to me is a soft word for thief—of being a dissembler, meaning liar. Of standing back and being amused by the world—i.e., being a bum. He makes a structure out of his weakness and claims it makes him a character, someone special. I can't support that. What is he? What has he? Life, health, an unhappy bride, peanut butter, and for all I know, drink and drugs. I don't even want to think about *that*. Not enough. *Ne suffit pas,* Jenny. And that's kept me sleepless ten thousand nights. Even so, now and then, I give him something."

"Sure. You sent him a check for fifty dollars a few months ago."

"You guys do your bookkeeping. I'd just gotten a check for a project review, a hundred dollars. I sent Jack half. I also gave him five hundred for Christmas. And I matched what he made when he had the waiter's job. When he worked, he made good money and didn't need anything from me. It's when he deliberately doesn't work that I won't give him what I give you and the others. I've worked full-time since I was twenty-one, and part-time since I was a kid. I believe in it. You've always worked."

"No, I haven't. There've been months and months when I lived off Oliver, and you sent me money."

"All right, a few months here or there. But Jack's had years. Idleness Fellowships. Gigolo Fellowships. Like Guggenheims."

"He's sacrificed lots of things in order to think through difficult problems. And he's fascinating about them. He writes beautiful things. You just don't know. You should listen to him sometimes. He can be more interesting about more things than anybody I've ever known."

"If he could only make a career of amusing his sister."

"It's not just me. He's got lots of friends. Lots of people find him fascinating. Everybody but you."

"Sometimes I do. But less and less."

"He knows that. He feels that. That's why he has to strain with you. If you'd only relax and enjoy each other as human beings."

"Sure. Like wardens and prisoners, Uncle Tom and Simon Legree. We're *not* just ordinary people to each other, we're *père et fils.*"

"Look at the examples you've chosen. Are you his warden? His overseer? Jesus, Dad."

I was getting tired, my tongue was tripping over itself. But it was not a time to give ground. "Look, he's my son and your brother. Our feelings toward him and each other are unbelievably complicated. But I think we both know what really counts here. His life is killing him—"

"Every life kills."

"Please don't interrupt."

"We've both interrupted. I was the one who—"

"Okay, it's this energy of discourse. Plato didn't write up his real dialogues. And we're both angry and 'Anger's the—' "

"—mode of reasoning.' Aristotle. You taught us that when we were ten. We've had great quotes from you, one for every mosquito bite."

"Conceded. But we're getting away from Jack. I believe he's gone over the hill. I saw it last night."

"Yes, when you told him he'd end up in prison. That was the worst, Dad."

"I didn't say that, Jenny. Though I confess I've been

scared to death he might. Slipping into it before he knew what he was doing. I'm scared everyone will leave him the way apparently Maria's left him. Maybe even his mother. Even you."

Her face drew together at this as if to lock in its loyalty. "Maria's an asshole."

"Maria aside, Jack's living off himself, by himself, for himself. He has nothing or no one to take care of but himself. If this selfishness is necessary armor for his high destiny, then I'm wrong and you're right. But I've had no evidence that says it is. All I see is a life formed around a wound. And don't think I haven't wondered if I'm not the one who inflicted it. And don't think I don't think all the time what I can do about it."

"Maybe it's too late for you to do anything."

"Jenny, as long as we're talking this way, I'm going to throw in something else. It's not just Jack's self-centeredness that's worried me. In some ways, you're the most generous and loving person I know, but it struck me that what you said about not wanting children because you think your life will shrivel up around them is self-centered in the same way Jack is." I could feel her tension here. Yet again, it was too late to stop. Even if the family pillars were going to crash. "Even now arguing with you or getting furious at Jack, life is astonishingly enriched, doubled, tripled by children. A family isn't just what the people you wrote about in your book make it out to be. I'm not saying it's not a terrific book. It's almost too terrific. There aren't just Gonerils and Regans and tyrant fathers and devouring mothers. I'm bewildered and pained that you yourself won't know the strangeness and beauty of it. I may be a selfish man, but there are parts of me that belong more to you and Jack and Ben and Livy than they do to me. Maybe I shouldn't be talking to you this way."

"Say anything you want, about me, Jack, anything."

"I'm frightened of a barrenness in both of you. And I wonder if it comes from some depth of resentment at me." I didn't look at her, only felt the heat of her tension near me. "Could I have wounded you so that you have to keep stuffing the wound with the world's tidbits? I take that back, I don't mean 'tidbits.' I know you're both serious, especially you, that you think hard and feel deeply about the most beautiful and difficult things. And that you, in any case, do something about them, tell students about them, write about them. You say Jack does too, but I've never seen a word of it. I don't know. Maybe this barrenness has less to do with you than with the times, the *Zeitgeist*." She was shaking her head a little, perhaps to see if it was still on. It had taken a lot for her to talk to me as she had, and I'd done the usual, the usual dump on her. Had taken over. "I may be wrong about everything. About one thing I'm not, though: Jack's very lucky he has you. You're his lifeline."

"No. He's his own lifeline."

"Right, but you're the one who believes in him most."

"But it's you he wants to believe in him, not me."

"I want to, but I can't now. I'm too philistine, I need a sign." She nodded, the nod a recognition that nothing had changed. We disagreed. We could go round and round about it, but it wasn't Indianapolis, there was no prize at the end. "We're exhausted," I said. I went down the hall and opened the door. I was too upset to kiss her. There was too much agitation between us. She, however, stepped toward me and raised her flushed head. That's all it took. Once again she was the little girl who had received good as well as bad from me. And I was happy kissing her cheek.

"How could you let her talk like that to you?" Emma's voice hovered between pitches as if it didn't know where to start or end. (That she herself had raked me over much hotter coals didn't count.) We were in rust-pocked Rufus, driving up and down the asphalt lanes of the green Midway, a common pacifier when we weren't up to walking. My legs had been giving me trouble. And we also drove because Rufus, groaning terribly in the last months of his metal-fatigued life, was a shell within the shell of Hyde Park. No one could hear us.

"Should I have slapped her?"

"No, but you could have said it wasn't right for her to talk to you like that. Doesn't she have any idea how much she and the rest of them mean to you? Any father I know would have shut her up. Or worse."

June was like early May this year, for, after a mild winter, there'd been a chill-raising spring. The green was full of metal highs, a kind of feverish fierce guilt as if it had to make up for what the crossed signals had suppressed. There were trees that had just started leafing, nerve-bare with just a froth of green. The air was full of maple pods spinning like tiny swallows—more like distant birds than little seeded boomerangs; and the white floral tents of horse chestnuts looked in their handsome depth like a field of tents. It was too beautiful to stay inside Rufus.

"Let's walk," I said. Emma parked near the statue of proud King Stanislas. "She was just trying to defend Jack. I can't get on her for that. She thinks he's Henry Miller, or some terrific poet-in-the-egg, who's being lashed by my burgher standards."

Arms around each other, we walked up Blackstone, past the handsome houses, Victorian, Queen Anne, French Provincial, Chicago brick, pseudo-Venetian, pseudo-Gothic, pseudo-inspirational. The pods spun around us. The air was delicious. Students were carrying boxes out of a residence hall; parents were packing them into cars. Books, stereos, hot plates, word processors, guitars, pots, duffel bags, goldfish bowls. The young were hugging and kissing each other good-bye; doors slammed, horns tooted farewell. It was four years since I'd driven Livy back from Ithaca. It seemed like twenty. We walked east on Fifty-seventh and turned south on Harper. My legs were tiring now, I felt sharp cramps around the knees. Emma was used to my leaning against walls or parked cars. Now I leaned against a golden Honda, just south of the last of the tiny cottages with their lawns and trees.

I said, "You told me that when your father died you burst out at your mother. You'd never been so angry at her."

"That's right. But who's dead?"

"Well, Agnes is going off for a long time. Longer than these kids have ever known. Of course, Jenny and Oliver were away for a couple of years, but this is different. It's upsetting them, and they may not even know why."

"Kids. You can't call them kids."

"No matter how old they are, these kids are still kids. And this is still what they call their family. It will be different when they have their own kids. This has been their nest, and now it isn't going to be. And old as they are, they're scared. Jack isn't going to have anyplace to come to between gigolo bouts and marriages. There I go again being mean to him."

"Not *to* him."

"Anyway, that's what I think's happening. The nest's on fire. Mama-bird's off. And who left Mama-bird so that she'd be free to be off, but Papa-bird? And who pushed them out of the nest but old Papa with all his talk about high mental life? A cheap substitute for fancy clothes, eastern schools, good cars, European vacations, and who knows, whatever they wanted."

All this was the rocks resettling after the little Jenny

earthquake. I actually felt pretty good. I was certainly no Lear being pelted by the storm. I was still sitting pretty. *Paterfamilias*. The four children, my little honor guard, my conspicuous contribution to the body politic. At one of the Christmas parties we all went to—odd that our half-Jewish family celebrated so intently the birth of that even odder half-Jewish child—a visiting Polish economist, a disciple of Mel Sorgmund's, came up to me at the buffet table as I was toothpicking meatballs into my mouth. "Everywhere I look this party I see hewch children. I hesk their names, each one says, 'Riemer.' I say I mast look their father, he mast half stim blawing out from nawstrils."

"Imagine her blaming you for pushing them toward the high mental life." Emma shook her little curls and stabbed her nose at me. (The long nose of northern people, which warmed the chill air before it shocked the brain.) "My God, if my father had read me Plato and explained Darwin to me, I'd have been at twenty what I'm not yet at thirty-five. I could have gone on to be something."

"She meant it just discontented them with so much, they couldn't be satisfied. I'd only tuned them in to play a few songs."

"Ridiculous. Did you become a butcher? Or a business-man? Wasn't that what your parents tuned *you* for?"

"Oh, no. Once my father heard me spell *Mississippi*, I was his little genius. He wasn't going to let this little arm cut pork chops. Anyway, once Grandpa Riemer died, I got enough bad messages about butchers to make me ashamed of the dear fellow. The way I told my friends about him, he sounded like Swift and Armour. As for mother, whatever she said looked wrong to me. No, it was easier for me than for my kids. I already occupied the world they were supposed to enter. Not that I was Copernicus or Shake-speare. There was plenty of room, and there still is, for them. Ben and Jenny are already way ahead of me, even with *Off My Chest*. Who knows? Maybe her trouble is, she's stumped for another book. Or still too tired out from *Wobbling Nucleus*. It did take her a long time."

"I hope she'll never forget how you praised it."

"Maybe that's the trouble. Maybe she feels guilty that she gets the praise and Jack the kicks in the rear."

"If you had that many excuses for not walking you'd never take another step."

I pushed myself off the little gold Honda. "Watch."

V

For more than five decades, my body had been a sort of silent—or sometimes exhilarated—partner. Now, like a reminder that my parental defense system was removed and that it was on the front line of the war everyone lost, it began shouting for attention. An orthopedist traced my leg cramps to the spurs of a disintegrating vertebra which snared the sciatic nerve; an internist showed me ghostly X rays of my stomach leaking through a diaphragmatic aperture into the chest. "A paresophagal hernia, Mr. Riemer. That's what's making us bilious and nauseous." *We* were to see if a fatless, spiceless diet would "do the trick." "Otherwise we might have to go the surgery route. Also we might get a mattesss which elevates the upper half of our body."

"I have a pine board under the mattresss now. For my back."

"That's fine for our lower half. We'll lick the upper with a tilter."

"I guess I'm lucky we don't have to dangle from a hook." We got a great kick out of that.

One day I woke up with my gums on fire. I couldn't remember the last time I'd had real dental trouble. All Schein and Riemer teeth were blessed. (Only Livy's braces and Agnes's root canal work had sent me into the financial pits of dentistry.)

My dentist, Oscar Spudde, presided over an office that was part assembly line, part Miami Beach. Patients got zipped along from hygienist to X-ray technician to the golden chair where Spudde himself assessed their mouths. The laughing receptionists, hygienists, technicians, took tropical dress cues from his Hawaiian slacks and sports shirts. The whole office swam in a resort, first name amiability. "Howya today, Cy? You *look* great. Jogging? No? You must be cutting down on the Mars Bars, you're getting so handsome we won't be able to concentrate on that mouth of yours."

Nonetheless, Spudde peered into it and trimmed his smile. "I don't like the look of that lower left side, Cy. I'm gonna send a full set of pictures down to the periodontist. There's bone loss there. Probably odontic infection, but I'm not gonna take a chance."

Ten little X-rays squares were clipped to a lit screen. Spudde pointed to a white spur stretched over a black valley between two snowy peaks. "It's not the absence of bone that worries me. It's that there's *some* bone there. I want Dr. Davies to look at it." The Floridian tan, the black eyes, huge in their skin-pink frames, the violently floral shirt, all seemed subdued by sympathy. I liked Spudde. As for those ancient-looking cliffs which were my teeth, they made me think of the new pictures of Saturn I had back on my desk, pucks of billion-year-old ice as remote from their native combustion as these calcium peaks from my pain.

Beyond the golden chair, Spudde's other patients moved in quest of cleaned mouths, filled cavities, extracted pain. "Hi, doc." "Howya doin', Cindy?" "You're lookin' good, Monty." I looked okay too. What did looks matter?

The next day, Spudde telephoned. "Dr. Davies wants a biopsy, Cy."

"Oh, God," I said. The word opened a door in me that had never been opened.

"I've made an appointment for you with Glisper. Head of oral surgery at Michael Reese. He's the best. Don't worry, kid. I'll be filling your teeth for decades. I'm eighty percent sure it's an infection." Eighty percent, which left twenty percent, a hole big enough to fall through and keep falling forever. "We have to face whatever music there is." *That* we meant a lot to me.

But there was heaviness in my eyes, pressure in my head, my cheeks twitched. That had never happened before. My body had had a terrible message and was on a hookup of its own. How could it have happened? Mother and Dad were scarcely dead, Dad at ninety-two, Mother at eighty-one. Little Orphan Cyrus was barely getting started. Was I going to be cheated out of my rightful longevity? What had I done? What had been done to me? What would Emma do? Darling Emma, she'd put everything she had into me. And the kids. No, they'd be *better* off. Should I call them? I could hear myself saying good-bye. I knew I was jumping ahead, making much of what was probably—please God—nothing. I might only lose some jaw. It would make me more attractive, trim some pig off my face. But sweating, heart knocking, I also knew something had rapped on the door.

* * *

Saturday, after I had added up the week's worth, I drove Emma's cranky Cutlass Supreme (swaggering name for so unsure a vehicle) uptown for the biopsy. It was an ugly day, lusterless and cold. Along the lake the trees looked like arthritic fingers. In addition to everything else, I was going to miss part of one of the NFL play-off games. These painless painkillers absorbed me, despite the monotonous sameness of the plays and commentary. When the Bears played great teams I could barely stand the tension of partisanship. The disciplined fury of the players, the collisions between their rage and their pieties, the verbal suppleness this produced in interviews fascinated me. Any great game was a joy and this one—the Cowboys and the Redskins—should be a knockout. Maybe I'd be back for the second half.

I drove past the Mestrovič Indians—my favorite sculpture in the world—to Michigan, past the Art Institute lions and into the Grant Park garage. There was space on the upper level near the Randolph Street entrance. Luck. The office was opposite the main library.

Glisper, stubby, gray, his kind features bunched in a large face, said he was delighted to see me. He told the nurses to set up for the biopsy, and after I was set with mouth tubes and protective sheets, he looked in my mouth and said, "I don't think there's all that much doing there." What a marvelous man. "Have you seen Dr. Davies?"

"No."

"Get Davies on the phone," he told the nurse.

I was spared. How lovely this office was. Gold and avocado were its colors. The throat of the rinsing bowl was deep gold, its curves were futuristic, beyond nature. Yet this odd room was intimate and cheerful. So were the nurses. Kind, patient, lithe. Maybe I'd only miss the first quarter.

Five minutes later, Glisper came back, drying his hands on a towel, his crowded face full of business. "Oh-*kay*. We'll go ahead with it." A needle pinged the inside of my cheek, and Glisper was off, lost in my mouth. From the wall, an orchestra played a muted *Ein Heldenleben*. Half my face had fallen away. (A hero's face.) I shut my eyes. Inside my mouth, there was heavy work, a distant tugging, cutting, ripping: not painful. Distant Glisper said, "While I'm in here, I'll take out that tooth. It keeps setting up infections for you." Gauze and cotton filled my dead mouth. "I'll send the tissue down to Davies. I don't think there's anything there. You'll hear one way or another in a couple of days. Tuesday we'll take the sutures out. Very nice meeting you."

Blessed physician with the good smile in the crowded face. "Thank you, Dr. Glisper."

At the drugstore downstairs, I picked up penicillin and Tylenol, and half an hour later, I lay on my bed in front of the play-off game. I had very little pain.

Tuesday, I took the I.C. uptown to have the sutures out. Glisper said, "The lab report's negative."

"Thank you, Dr. Glisper."

He went back to his marvelous work, and I back south. Eased. Intact. Immune. Almost, almost immortal.

In the train rollicking south along the beautiful green lake, I was suddenly, strangely gripped by a need I couldn't identify. The speaker announced, "Hyde Park ne-ext." I got up, waited at the door while we passed the Fifty-fifth Street shopping center. The door opened. I got out and walked in the clear morning toward the exit. Then I realized what I wanted. It was to see, to embrace and hold, my children.

With Agnes thousands of miles away in a village too remote to be easily phoned, where even mail took weeks to arrive, the endless family involvement—birthdays, Mother's Days, Valentine's Days, the plane trips "home," the weekly phone calls about everyone's doings—slackened. Agnes's silent authority had been the family glue. Nothing replaced it. We were still in touch, still loving, but what had surfaced in Jenny now surfaced elsewhere. Our family joshing had harsher notes. Ben had studied and was writing about the physiological and psychological malignance of fetal life, but now he had a family of his own, which floated benignly over such horror. He and Nancy looked up a justice of the peace in the country and got married one weekend. "We didn't see any point in having a big to-do." Perhaps under Jenny's tutelage, he decided that his ease masked resentment of paternal tyranny. "Damn, Dad. Please don't always tell me what to do. I've got a wife for that." It was not much of a protest, but more than I'd heard from him.

As for Livy, worry about her mother, salted by years of exasperation at her, was redirected into questioning my worth, my advice. "I know how to handle it, Dad. I've spent three years being the law. Can you say as much?" I was taken aback by this too, though once again thought the source of it was the children's sense of loss. So grown-up, yet so dependent.

There was a new and uneasy mix in me as well; it also had to do with freedom from family and new obligation to it. It started the night Ben called to tell me Nancy was pregnant. (I think it was ten minutes after she told him.) "Ben, it's marvelous. I'm thrilled. Overwhelmed."

"You sound more excited than we are." But his cool was streaked with excitement at my excitement.

"When did you find out?"

"Today. I thought you'd want to know right off."

"I do indeed. I'm very grateful, Benny. Give Nancy my love. What a fine, big child it's going to be. When will it arrive?"

"She thinks she's about six weeks into it."

"That gives us all time to prepare."

My father had been forty when I was born, his father thirty-eight when he'd been, so my image of a grandfather was an eighty-year-old man with white hair and mustache. Though the mirror never failed to surprise me with the aged fellow who looked back from it, that fellow was still far from white hair. Yet I was going to be "Grandpa." Fine, okay, but clearly another stage of decrepitude. And of obligation. It had been years since I'd worried about small children being sick, hurt, lost, unhappy, years since I'd worried about paying for their well-being, their tuition. Now, despite the filter of Ben and Nancy, that was going to happen again. I felt it already.

"I better start putting a little money away for the baby," I told Emma. "By the time he's in college, tuition'll be fifty thousand a year."

"I imagine Ben will take care of that. You did."

"Ben's work is uncertain, his head is in the archives. He'll never have a nickel."

It was such unrest that sent me to a reluctant and admonitory Seldon. "I want to make a little money, Sel."

"I thought Mother Riemer had left you in clover."

"She did well enough by me, but what will these dollars mean twenty years from now?"

"Cy, commodities aren't for types like you. I don't care how many grandchildren you think you have to make rich."

"It's not a question of 'rich.' I don't want to be rich."

"I see. You just want to play games. All right, I'll take your dough. But don't come weeping."

"I don't want to lose, just to make a little quicker than you make it in the stock market. I'm willing to risk a little for that."

"A little isn't enough down here. It's not playing footsie with IBM. You're in for real or you're not."

"I trust you, Sel."

"Don't. I'm not going to cheat you—"

"That's what I mean. My broker's a dummy. Everything he touches melts away. To me, broker means 'broke.' I'll try this."

The quickest, steepest plunge of my life. In two weeks, I lost more money than I'd saved in five decades. I wasn't poor, but by the time I took off to see the kids that spring, I'd lost a third of what mother had left me. It was like an auto-da-fé. I'd gone nuts, piled the goods of my life into a pyre and ignited them. "How could I have done it?" I asked Emma.

"You wanted too much. Wanted to be a prince and leave your heirs princes. Instead of just taking care of what you have right here."

"How did I know Reaganomics were going to hit the fan? Everybody rich is supposed to get richer now. That was the whole idea."

"You should never have trusted Seldon. You know he's a downer. And he'd lose your money first. He resents you." I was too low to contradict this. "You should have stuck with B.J." Billy Jugiello's Christmas card this year showed a picture of a Jugiello trinity: Billy, Priscilla, and infant Billy. Jugiello was every bit as large as I'd pictured him, but he was bald as a billiard ball; in fact the eight ball, for the biggest surprise was that he was black.

"He hasn't called in months. He's sparing my feelings."

"You call him."

I rang him up. "Doctor, good to hear your voice. I thought I'd lost you. Must have called you fifty times. Someone around here said he saw in the paper you'd written a book. That right?"

Usually, I was so elated that anyone had heard anything at all about the book that I couldn't think of anything else. Now, though, with my money washing away, I said, "That's right Billy, but I'm not calling about literature. I want you to make some money for me."

"Doctor, I wish I could. If you were a short-seller, I'd have made money for you, but you're a meat and potatoes man. You like to see everything on the plate. There's still some nice Municipal Unit Trusts."

"I'm not looking for shelters, Billy. I'm looking for something to shelter."

"Well, you know, Doc, smart money buys when the market's low. Everything's underpriced."

"Sure, Billy," I said. "That's what you've been telling all us sailors."

"Please don't despise me, Doc," said Billy. "I'm proud of having a man like you, an author, for my client. I tell everyone about it."

"Oh, Billy, what a thing to say." He made me feel like Einstein. If it was a snow job, it was good snow. "I didn't think that was one of your interests."

"No, Doc, I want to improve myself. I even thought of ordering your book. I just haven't had a minute."

"If you'll really read the book, I'll send you a copy."

"Jesus, Doc, that would be great. Sure I'll read it. If I can understand it all. And I don't want you to send it. I'm going to write it down right now. Could you give me the name?"

I gave it to him. "Sorry I snapped at you, Billy."

"Nothing to it, Doc. And don't worry. Things'll turn around."

After that talk, I put *Ella Fitzgerald Sings Gershwin* on the stereo, and took a Christmas cigar, a bottle of American Chablis—I was back to cheaper wine—and the *Tribune* out to the porch. A thirteen-year-old shot four schoolmates with the rifle Daddy gave her for Christmas; judges were caught fixing cases in the Graylord Scam; a chop shop was broken up half a mile from where I sat; a hundred kilos of cocaine were found in a two-ton wrecked on the Dan Ryan Expressway; President Reagan assured communicants of "every other religion" that they were "free to practice in our country"; cases of wife and child abuse had tripled in the last year; the Institute of World Conflict reported that "four million men are presently engaged in fighting forty-two wars on five continents." The usual God's-in-his-heaven news.

Between two slats of porch rail, by my blue lounger, was a spider's web. In the oval center, two white eyeish dots looked at me. "Hello, pal," I said. "How's the market in Spiderville?" A breeze parasoled the web. "Hold on, pal." In his oval, Spider held. "They're trying to break our hearts, pal." I filled a glass with gold stuff and tipped it his way: "Here's looking at you." Ella Fitzgerald sang "Fascinating Rhythm." I lit a black cigar—a contraband from Havana packaged by Davidoff et Cie in Geneva, sent for Christmas by Mel Sorgmund. I watched the tip swell into ash fur. "Look at this, pal," holding it where Spider could see it. He scuttled away like crazy to the edge of the web. "Oh, boy. What a dope I am. Forgive your thoughtless pal. He's not A-1 these days."

"You've had a bad time."

"I'm going down the tube. My teeth, my money."

"You take things too hard," said Spider. He'd scuttled back to the oval center. *"Relax. Go see your kids."*

Four planes in three days. First, Midway to Saint Louis. Emma took me to International House for the C & W limousine. "Give the kids my love and have a good time." She was off to see Dr. Wanny—she'd been feeling dizzy—then on to her new interior decorating classes at the Merchandise Mart.

Livy met me at the Saint Louis airport in her new Mustang. This was her first post-training assignment with the FBI. She showed me her revolver, her "knuckle-breaker"—an innocent looking little scrolled bar—a recording device inside a compact, a camera inside a lipstick. "What a wonderful world, Livy. Every object's in the information business." Her eyes were as clear and beautiful as ever, but her face looked a little sharper, a little older. Was some of the bloom already off this rose? We drove to her apartment in Clayton; it was sunny and pretty. "No plants or animals," she said. "I can't tell when I'll be out of town for a week."

"Is the work hard, honey?"

"A lot of it's paperwork. But a lot's interesting. And I'm glad not to be working all the time with people who are finished before they start."

We walked around the zoo, went to the aviary and the art museum, then drove down to the river and rode through the beautiful Saarinen arch. "I haven't done any of this, Daddy. I'm so glad you came. I'm having a great time." I said I was too, which was true, but still there was that little shadow in her face centered somewhere around the little lump of reset nose. To me it said that my daughter's life was moving from A.M. to P.M. before she knew it.

"Any love in your life these days, sweetie?"

"I hope I'll be able to convince a man there's more to me than a gun and a pair of handcuffs."

"It's not a gun that makes you irresistible."

"You're still all sunshine, Daddy."

When she drove me to the airport the next morning, I could hardly bear to say good-bye to her.

Both Jenny and Ben were in Washington now. Ben was doing research at the Federal Reserve. A few hours a week he worked on his own book at the Library of Congress. "How's it coming along?" I asked him.

A Livy-like shadow came into his face. "I don't know if I'll ever bring it off."

"Of course you will," I said. "Persistence, that's all that counts. The 'long patience,' Flaubert called it."

Nancy was enormous with my grandchild. Verg, who'd allowed himself to be transferred to Ben when Agnes took off for Rwanda, was, said Ben, "being psyched up for the baby. He'll let us keep it if it doesn't cry too much." There was lots of Debussy, Rameau, and Ravel on their stereo. Nancy said, "Ben says French music is right for an intellectual fetus."

Jenny came over, and the four of us went to La Plaza, a Spanish restaurant on Columbia. (Oliver had a class in Malay; his next assignment was Kuala Lumpur.) I felt the slightest distance between Jenny and me and attributed it to the prominence of Nancy's belly. Very slight. When I said good-bye to her, once again I could hardly bear it. Ben, Jenny, and soon, a new Riemer. Mine and not mine. Even more: almost me. Yet, with the tender sting of good-bye, there was also relief. Feeling was a chain.

The third plane rode up the spine of Manhattan, a celestial version of the buses I used to take north from Stuyvesant High School. Manhattan looked like a slice of liver Daddy had cut out of a cold steer. Somewhere below, in one of the cells, was Jack.

Jenny had given me his address, a brownstone on Seventy-fourth between Riverside and West End. I'd written in advance I was coming, no guarantee he'd be there, but he was, five flights up a stairwell that stank of old varnish and old meat. "Unpleasant, isn't it?" he called down. "I can't get used to it. It's like a dead cat's guts. Can you make it? I'd send the Saint Bernard down with the booze, but he's on strike."

"Well, if I don't make it, at least I've heard you, which is a relief."

He was on the landing, arm out, smiling, dressed as I'd seen him a year ago in Chicago, in the Riverside Drivers baseball cap, an acrylic-streaked T-shirt, and torn denims. "You've put on weight, Jack." I took his hand.

"Bloat," he said cheerily. "Weather's been lousy. I haven't jogged, even walked. Nothing to do but eat and read. Come in."

In. What to say? Bare, bright, geometric, furnished by Monsieur Rien. A cave was better furnished. When I stopped blinking at the light bursting through the un-shaded window, I saw a mattress on the floor, blankets on it, one bunched for a pillow. One chair—no, not a chair, a stool. On it the portable Remington he'd had since high school. On the floor, a pile of typed pages and some paperbacks; by the mattress, a jar of peanut buter and a half loaf of Wonder Bread. I could see a toilet, and a sink behind a door; no sign of a kitchen. There was a closet. I opened it: a gray suit on a hanger, a sleeveless down jacket on a nail, a sweater and two dress shirts hanging from a broom. On the floor, a quarter-size refrigerator. I opened it: a gallon carton of milk, a bottle of vitamin pills, a carton of Baby Ruths.

"Inspection satisfactory?"

"Sure," I said, trying to smile back. As if I were watching Jack playing a role in *The Lower Depths*.

"Maybe I should have met you downstairs," he said. "But I know you wanted to see where I operated."

I refrained from picking up the odd participle to say he seemed more operated on than operator, and said only, "I don't know what to say."

"It's better than it looks. It's fine. What does a person need?"

"Right. You're right. Thoreau. Gandhi. Why mess with superfluity?"

"I'm happy here. Or I can be, long as I have something to read and don't have to think about myself."

"I don't see any reading light. How do you read at night? By the overhead light?"

"Sure, it's fine. I'll be making some money soon. Then I'll buy a good light."

"How long have—"

"A couple of months. Since I left Sondra's. It's a good deal. I sublet from a guy who's never lived here. He's gonna use it for an office when he gets enough money to buy the system he wants. He gives it to me for what it costs him, three hundred bucks a month." I stopped myself from saying, "A jail cell would be cheaper and better furnished."

"I owe him a little."

"How much?"

"Six hundred. But I've got something cooking. I'm going to make a lot of dough."

Some weight lifted from my innards. Even if it was just one of Jack's inventions, the direction was right. "Doing what?"

"No point in telling you now. Just some dumb TV scheme I cooked up. I'll learn if it works out next week. Then I'll tell you. It's not worth talking about."

I know that. I'd heard about such schemes for years. "Do you have some money now? Enough to eat on?" I pointed to the peanut butter.

"I'm not rolling in it, but I'm all right. There's no point paying the rent till I have some real dough. He won't kick me out. Or if he does, it'll take a while. I have my eye on another place." (Like a fugitive who always knows where the exits are.) "It wouldn't take me too long to move. What's the matter, Dad?"

I guess I had my hand on my forehead. I was a little dizzy. I said, "This isn't good, Jack."

"Look," he said. "Why don't we take off? Have you had lunch? I mean I could give you a peanut butter sandwich, but—"

I wasn't hungry, I'd had a sandwich at National Airport, but of course I said, "No. Let's get something. The nicest place around."

"Great. We'll go up to Amsterdam." He opened the door. I stopped myself from asking if he didn't want to change, not necessarily into coat and tie, but at least a dress shirt and an untorn pair of pants. But what did that have to do with what counted here?

It was a relief to get out: out of this empty cube and out of the tenement.

Jack too seemed relieved. He took in the gaseous air blown up from the Hudson as if it were champagne. West End Avenue offered another vintage. And Broadway, that was fifty-year-old Chateau Lafite.

Jack's street walk was as contrived as a goosestep, a sort of linebacker's hunched roll. I suppose the idea was to intimidate tough guys. Though what could any of them get from him except the standard pleasures of demolition? (A scared boy hid in that walk.) At the Broadway light, I took his arm at the elbow. He allowed this for about five seconds then did his strut across the street. On Amsterdam he checked outside menus. "No, you won't like this place."

"Any place is fine with me, Jack."

Not with him though. After four blocks, I said, "How about this place?"

"Fine," he said. "Just the one I was going to pick."

It was a little Italian place with checkered tablecloths and candles in fat Chianti bottles. At this tail end of lunchtime, it was nearly empty.

Seated, Jack was at ease. Or more, he was Henry VIII at Windsor: in charge, money and waiters at his command. I suppose the grand manner was intended to compensate for the baseball cap, T-shirt, and torn denims; of course aristocrats should be recognized in rags. He looked at the menu the way a scholar does a manuscript, then ordered a dozen *moules,* a lobster bisque, filet mignon, a big salad. "I'll wait on dessert. May I pick us out a little wine, Dad?"

"Wish you would, Jack." Thank God he was on top of something. I ordered a chicken sandwich, and he a forty-dollar bottle of Bordeaux.

For the next hour I watched him eat and drink with that semioblivious rapture you see in animals, lost in what they're transforming into themselves.

He was what he chewed. This was done noisily, along with grunts, snaps, and snorts, quite a range of dental and nasal percussion. I almost felt I was passing through his teeth and guts. I'd read of concentration camp victims who died as they ate their first meal—their first bite!—in liberation; but of course they'd been starving. Jack just turned into his teeth. This meal was like a career for him.

In the first real pause, he looked up and said, "It doesn't look it, but my stomach's shrunk. I can't eat the way I used to."

I looked at him, greased and bloodied, and burst out

laughing. He did too. That was better. "If they give a Ph.D. in eating, Jack, you're in. Outside of the zoo, I've never seen such absorption."

"No," he said, smiling. "Not the same. Food's much more for me. I remember a piece in the *News-Letter* on the difference between animal and human appetites."

"Yes," I said. "On the after-effects of endocrine stimulation. A very good piece. Amazing that you remember it."

"Oh, I've thought a lot about it. Because it said that was what enabled human beings to have coherent emotional lives, memory, symbols, rituals, all this"—spreading his hands, one with a fork, one with a knife, showing the restaurant, the wine, the candles. "It's an important article. I think I'll get a little dessert if that's okay, Dad."

"You know your limits."

"Unfortunately I do."

I switched to something else. "I've been worried about you. I got this somewhat overwrought letter from Sondra Bieber. She said she got back to her place and found it in— pretty bad shape."

"She's a sad, mad dummy." His tart arrived; he tore into its creamy, fruited heart.

"You didn't always think so. Apparently, there was a huge phone bill."

He waved his empty coffee cup at the waiter, then took a long swallow of the red wine. "She knows I'll pay her. I was all messed up about Maria. She was in Bangkok one day, Cairo next. I hated her like crazy one minute, missed her like crazy the next. I tried to settle it in phone calls. Look, when I make some money—and I'll be doing that soon—I'll settle with Sondra." There were drops under his eyelids and hairline, his face was pinking and paling, his breath heavy.

"What sort of project is it, Jack?" I thought that

perhaps, now that he was fed, he'd open up. Maybe there was something.

But no, his answer was the usual one.

"No point in talking about it. Once it comes through I'll tell you. A little Armagnac would be a topper on this feast."

"Why don't we get out of here, get a little air, take a little walk? I think your system's in overdrive as it is."

"I wish that were my trouble."

"What is the trouble?"

He looked down at the empty plate, held up a minute, then said, "The only thing I want to do is the only thing I can't."

"What is that?"

"You know, philosophy. Old-line philosophy. The big questions. They're so deceptive, they seem so easy. Like going for a walk, you're on your way, nothing to it, but before you know it, you're not quite where you thought you were. You take a left here, a right there, and all of a sudden you know you don't know where you are. You're lost, so lost you know you'll never get out."

"Jack, the greatest intelligences have cracked up on these things. How can you take it so personally?"

"That's what I'm about. What I want to be about. Everything else is simple for me, boring, doesn't count."

Was this cooked up to keep me from finding out what really made him tick? His latest excuse for not doing anything? Could it be true? Even partially true? "Maybe if you started doing something else, the sheer activity would carry over into philosophy. Energy spillover or something."

"Yeah, I made great philosophic strides down at the Commodity Exchange."

"Well, you're not making any kind now."

"That's right, I'm not. I sleep, I walk, I eat—more or

less—I read, I look at people. Every day's another installment of nothing. Enough. I'm making too much of it. You
brought good weather, you treated me to a great feast, life
isn't so bad."

"How about a friend, Jack? You've always had a friend.
Or Maria."

"Yeah, that's always been easy for me. But Maria's worn
out that part of me. For a while. The way working in the
Exchange wore down other things. Everybody has to respect
himself. After a while, I couldn't take it down there; and I
couldn't take it with Maria. Did you know she was Dochel's
cast-off? Your pal's garbage?"

"What? You're crazy, Jack. That's wrong."

"Oh, I don't care. That wasn't what did it."

"But not Seldon, Jack. Probably no one, but if anyone,
more likely your friend Felix. You said his ex-girl friends
were all over the office."

"Hell no, she was too smart to join that band. No, she
went for the kook. She's a savior. That's why she went for
me. I was another repair job. Trouble's what she lives for.
But she doesn't stay with it. Too smart for that. A month of
Dochel leaves a lot of stink on the bones. I don't mean that
did it for me, though the idea of that old guy's lips on her
parts—I can't talk about it. Who needs her, anyway? All
that cold brain and pushing. Like living with an electrical
storm. A high price to pay for coition. No matter how fast I
moved, compared to her I was always standing still. When
she went off to sow her poppa's money around the world, I
was happy. I ran into Sondra, she needed someone to baby-
sit her plants. I thought, here's my chance, I'll really get
something done now. Of course, nothing happened. I
thought it was missing Maria. I did miss her. You live next
to a volcano, you need that rumble. I used to wake up at
two in the morning and call her in Hong Kong or Nairobi.

And we'd start arguing, long distance. That's when she came out with this Dochel garbage. Among other things. Ten thousand miles away. I got so sick. Really sick. I had diarrhea in my pants. I slept in it on the floor. God knows what else I did. I was out of my head." *Oh, Sondra, we Riemers don't. Not our style.* "Speaking of which, excuse me."

I paid the check and waited for him at the door. We were the last lunch customers. Just as well. Jack was not a sight decent restaurants like to exhibit. Even relieved, he was still heaving, swallowing, putting the pinch on his body. (What an expressive medium his digestive tract was.)

"Are you sick? Would you like to lie down?"

"I want to get out, walk it off. It was a great *bouffe.*"

We walked north. Amsterdam hadn't changed much since my boyhood. These buildings were deeper in me than any others: the little public library on Eighty-second where I read so many terrifying fairy stories mother tried to keep me from going there. Barney Greenglass, the Sturgeon King, still sat off Eighty-sixth. But Riemer's Fine Meats hadn't left a trace. There was a bathroom appliance place there, full of shy pink sinks and sherbet-colored toilet seats. Up the street was our old apartment. I didn't want to pass it; I had to be alone for that. I didn't want Jack to intrude his idea of my feelings on them. There were too many of them here anyway. All over New York blocks were totally transformed, but these blocks had stayed like an emotional trap for me. I knew the fire hydrants, the cracks in the sidewalk, the grain of walls I'd played handball against forty-five years ago with Fiskie, Larry, Dum-Dum, Phil. Whenever I walked here, or east to Columbus, west to Broadway, there was too much: Mr. Brittain with his eyepiece examining my watch; the steam, naptha, and big drums of French's Cleaners; the American twist bread in Cushman's window—how mother loved it; Eddy, the rival butcher; Ciro's Fruits, the pears and nectarines glowing between cardboard pommels; the Brewster (where Uncle Milton lived) and the Peter Stuyvesant (where I once saw Artur Schnabel); the Schuyler Theater, which became El Colon in the fifties. These were all gone, and so was the Columbus Avenue el, which came down during the war and opened the dark streets to extraordinary light.

We turned down Eighty-sixth to Broadway. A Camaro's theft alarm screamed for help. (Cursed devices, which punished only bystanders.) Jack, no longer rolling, heaved himself along, but belched less; his system was making some sort of truce with his consumption. "Jack, dear," I said, "I wonder if a talk with a professional, a therapist of some sort, might help you. Unlock you. Or do they say 'unblock' you? I'd very much like to pay for that."

"You've made that offer before. Is it important for you?"

"That you're in good shape? Yes. Of course."

"You called grandma a hypocrite because she was always after you for 'your own good.' "

"You keep a good record." Too good. Which is why he needed help. "I shouldn't've."

"Why not? She was other things too. Everybody's a hypocrite. Saints, everybody. I looked it up."

"What?"

"*Hypo,* 'under'; *krites,* 'judge.' Under the judge. An actor."

Like father. Taking no wooden-nickel words. Still huffing, but in there swinging. The verbal fifteen-rounder. I wasn't in a fighting mood. Still. "If you're your own judge, you're not just an actor."

"Acting's not bad."

"Right. That's my hope, that you'll swing into action. That's what a doctor can help with."

"Maybe. I've thought of it. I've thought of everything.

On the couch, just letting rip. 'I dreamed. I saw. I think. I did. I didn't.' I. I. I. I. I. I. You think I'd like that?"

"Anybody would."

"But that's all I've done in my life. I'm sick of it. I hate the word *I*. I looked it up once, all the *I* words: *je, ich, yo, ya, wó, ah, eu.* Every ugly syllable the mouth can make."

"*Ego.* Two syllables."

"Got me. Another beauty. None ugly as *I*. Mulebray *I*. Even looks ugly, snooty little prick, all by itself, so full of itself."

"Whew. Too much, Jack. It's what we're given. It's not our fault. Maybe therapy takes away its ugliness."

"Maybe. But I'm not going to ask you for anything."

"You're not asking. It's something I want. For the part of me that's you. My *I* in you."

"I think I'll refuse anything. Except what's too much for you to give."

What in hell did that mean? I looked at the little-boy features stuck in the swelling and retracting flesh, the dumb baseball cap and T-shirt, the offensive rip at the knee. We were in front of a candy store; a ziggurat of peanut brittle filled the window. A favorite Riemer treat. Not now. "I don't understand. You just want my refusal? Why is that important to you? I mean is it more important than getting out of the bind you're in?"

The middle of Broadway was the same *schmutzig* strip of grass, end-stopped with benches filled with old geezers. Pulled out of bins of Geezerdom to replace those who'd sat there when I was a kid. New York's necessary quota of decrepitude.

"Maybe so," said Jack.

This was no answer. Was he married to Refusal? To Nothing? Was that the idea now? I couldn't let it go at that. North and south, the movie theaters or my childhood,

Yorktown and Thalia, Loew's 83rd, still there, but four theaters, RKO 81st—gone. *Under Two Flags, The Awful Truth, Top Hat,* Jean Hersholt delivering the Dionne quintuplets. Hundreds of them filling my head. I couldn't throw my son into the *schmutz* of Broadway. "If your TV contract, or whatever you're waiting for, doesn't come through, would a thousand bucks or two, and maybe six hundred to pay the rent you owe, be enough to set you up for a job hunt?"

He stopped in the street and faced me, much too dramatic for my taste with people walking by left and right. The little boy's face on the large body had a man's coldness in it now. "Face it, Dad. I'm finished. I'n never going to be what you want me to be. You can't buy it for me. I can't get it my own way either. Whether you meant it—however you meant it, I appreciate it. But it's beside the point. We missed the train. I'm going to take off. You take care."

He put out his hand. Confused, I put both mine on his arms. To hold him. He moved back. I stretched and kissed him on the cheek. He smiled—I don't know what was in the smile—and took off with a heavy trot. At Eightieth, he crossed to the west side, and I lost sight of him.

I read somewhere how Indians fished in frozen lakes. They cut a hole in the ice, then banged on the adjacent ice with rocks. This created pressure, which stunned the fish; they rose to the surface and were scooped up. On Broadway, in air that felt not like ice but the inside of a carburetor, I found myself gasping in the street.

One thing you can't do on an American city street is nothing. You can't stand still. (Unless you want to be noticed, which few do.) I must have stood on Broadway a minute or more before I noticed I was being noticed. And noticed, too, that "No, Jack's" and "Oh, Jack's" were on my lips as well as in my head. Half of me was going after him, but I wasn't. I think I took a few steps and felt sciatic pain shooting up my left leg. For relief, and also to get hold of myself, I hoisted the leg on a fire hydrant, leaned over and tied my shoe. That was noticeable, but understood and permitted. The pain eased. I walked to Seventy-ninth and crossed to the median strip to sit with other woeful ancients on a bench. The only place was next to a malodorous tramp, a real stinker. I didn't move. The stink—some foul chlorophyll drawn by fierce chemical dissolution of harsh food and augmented by the staleness of resignation, illness, carelessness, *whatever*—somehow objectified my state of mind, externalized and made it real. In me, a sort of Doppler effect had set in: the farther away Jack got, the sharper the pain he left in me. For a while anyway, he'd become what I'd warned him about. Self-fulfilling prophecy? Was I really the lion in his street?

No, he was his own lion. He saw that, said that. But that was it. He did nothing about it. He'd thrown in the towel. *Il gran rifiuto.* He'd made a grand refusal. That was somewhere in the *Inferno,* in the canto with those who'd lost the use of their intellects, who'd cursed their parents, their ancestry, their birth, the human species itself. Suddenly I was hungry to see the actual words on the page, some terrific wisdom with which to handle this agitation. If my leg would hold up, I could walk down to Rizzoli's. But Jack wasn't cursing anyone. Self-annihilation wasn't cursing. And verbal suicide wasn't suicide. No matter now much truth there was, it was still rhetoric. Which meant justification more than description. Or a punishment for me.

Someone said tragedy was a way of justifying misery as necessity. Jack had eaten, he'd feasted, he'd lost himself in stuff; his system, already strained, strained some more. He wasn't a tragic figure. He wasn't lost. Only for now, and maybe to me. When I was covering neighborhoods for the City News Bureau, the black term for insurance arson was "Jewish lightning." I was contending with my own form of Jewish lightning. Jack had set himself on fire, like the Buddhist monks in Vietnam. It was dramatic protest, a way of getting what they wanted. Jack had made a bonfire of himself before his father.

Il gran rifiuto. No, that was too grand for Jack. *Il piccolo rifiuto.* His resignation wasn't a curse against generation and species. It was words. No matter how true it felt to him, the words made a stand, a declaration, a poem of himself. The self was operating, advancing itself. The retreat was an advance. His misery was an assertion of superiority. Losing oneself to have oneself, to augment oneself, to guarantee what was greater than the rotten self one's idleness and self-reproach created. Van Gogh said he'd accepted the role of a madman as Degas did that of a notary public. Jack played the role of Failure. Yet van Gogh was part madman; and Jack was at least partly what he said he was.

I pushed off the bench. Why stew beside the stewed stinker? I'd walk down to Rizzoli's to find Dante, read the canto, and pull myself out of unhappiness with the help of genius. Wasn't that what it was for? If my leg would hold up.

A cough. The tramp, the stinker, was trying to get my attention. He wasn't an ancient. Wrong about that too. He had young eyes, and there was young flesh beneath the grizzle. His eyes were hazel, almost Livy's color, but unlike Livy's, set back in a web of vein like an animal in ambush. Did he want something? Money?

Why not? I took a ten, no, all out, a twenty from my wallet, studied it for a second—the pugnacity of Andrew Jackson under the whipped curl of his white hair, his Roman senator disdain—and handed it over. The stinker's arms—in a denim shirt long past color—stayed by his knees. The hell with it. I reclaimed the twenty.

How much was one supposed to do? I looked away from his surprise and crossed Broadway. Not to Jack's side, but the east.

I usually enjoy flying, the motion and busyness of flight, packing up, checking out, taxiing to the airport, waiting, boarding, the flight itself, the take-off, the view of the city, the clouds, and the diversions: announcements, drinks, snacks, then the preparations for landing, the canny annihilation of time in the instrument that annihilates it best. This spiral of defiance to earthbound metabolism exhilarates me. The gold and silver air, the blue purity of the atmosphere, my fellow passengers, fifty, a hundred, two or four hundred people I'd never see again, or notice if I did, transformed into mates by this release from gravity in unnatural transportation. Even those who plunge into their normality and work in shirtsleeves over papers in their briefcase, absorb, or, at least, divert me. But on this flight back to Chicago, I was not cheery.

My habit is to get to airports an hour before departure. I like to be first in line for seat assignments. Not this time.

I'd had a bad night. Six or eight times I got dressed and started off for Jack's. Twice I got to the hotel lobby before coming back. Here I was, in Jack's city, separated from him by less than a mile, less than half a mile. I must go to him, tell him he was not what he said he was. That I was not what he thought I was, or, if I was, he must ignore me. I'd offer him money. "Get away a while, Jack. Motion itself is good for you. You could go to Maria. Or just get away to think things out in a new place. Colorado, Switzerland, some island, Paris. Buy yourself some new clothes. Remake the outside, the inside'll follow." Or again, "You should talk things out with a professional. You don't really know yourself. Which may be all right, but it's doing you in. You've got to turn yourself around." But in the lobby, or at the door of my room, I stopped, retreated, got undressed, got back into bed and, to stop thinking, turned on the television. I could take nothing in. I tried to read. No go. Nor could I sleep. The last time, I found channel J and forced my appetite along its lines. I managed to get some sleep after that, two or three hours. I woke to the chill babble of a morning news show and fell asleep again. I woke an hour before plane time. Panic. I threw my stuff in a bag, made a scene at the check-out desk—"I can't wait, take the card now or I'll leave"—urged my cab driver to give it the gun and arrived at LaGuardia with ten minutes to spare.

I had to choose between a middle seat or one in the smoking section. Better cramps than cancer.

In the window seat was a stubby old dame in a black dress who turned the pages of a little book thickened with paste-ins of saints. Over it, she muttered some Neapolitan susurrus of imploration. I read a *Newsweek* account of a film in which the world was taken over by telekinetic children. (Was the world frightened of its children?) My other neighbor passed me the plastic glass of perforated ice cubes and the little bottle of scotch I'd ordered. (It had been years since I'd ordered whisky on a flight.) A dark-haired woman with black eyes and a good smile. Thirtyish, attractive. I asked her if she'd like the *Newsweek*. No, she said, she read *Time* and that was her week's quota of the world. The smile was really fine, she had beautiful, full lips. I seldom talk to people on planes, but she clearly wanted to talk and I, apparently, wanted to listen. She was going to visit her father in Chicago. No ordinary visit. He was ill, and she was going to get him to talk into a tape recorder about his life. "I'll have his voice. His life." There was the slightest break in her voice, the slightest inclination of her head as if she were registering in advance the blow that was coming, perhaps inoculating herself by submitting to a premonition of it. I was conscious of warmth coming from her arm into mine as they lay beside each other on the padded seat rest. It vivified my interest in her story. Now I withdrew a fraction of an inch. Another note had sounded, one which scooped its fish from another part of that grab bag we call the "heart."

Filial devotion. Which I had at the beginning and end of my parents' lives, and had even more strongly now that they weren't around to interfere with it. The shift from sexual excitement to this retrospection confused me. (Only human beings who go against the deepest grain of human society fuse such feelings. The rest of us shy off, quickly, from anything which comes remotely close to the fusion. I'm sure I never had an incestuous thought in my life, though I grant this assurance may be the freeze laid on the wildness beneath.)

I still had plenty of life in me, I hadn't felt its limits, thought little of death, and, when I did, without terror— though this may be another trick consciousness worked on the wilderness. The children weren't *my* future. I wanted to be in charge of that for a while. But did they have to shadow that *while?* Why wasn't Jack simple, straight, devoted, filial in the way this woman was?

The plane, our little time capsule, began its descent over the blazing lake. It cut the suburban shore and sliced over houses, factories, and the ribbon roads around O'Hare.

As we locked into the vermicular walk-off, I said, "I hope you'll find your father better than you fear."

There was a twenty-minute wait for the C & W limousine to Hyde Park, so I took a cab. I watched the city accumulate around me, the bedazzled cubes and cylinders of the airport's feeder hotels, the automotive dreck—stations, accessories and parts stores— the crimson brick and pale knobs of the Polish churches standing over neighborhoods abandoned by their congregations, the back of the Loop, surprised, trousers down at its knees.

"You're back."

"Yes. Where are you?"

"On the porch. Here I come." Running down the hall, in shorts, barefoot, her face lit up. A kiss. "How was it? How's the Riemersphere?"

"Let me change, I'll tell you everything. Lots to tell. Not all of it bad. A spritzer would taste great."

When I came out and sat in the blue lounger, the wine glass, full of gold bubbles, was on the windowsill. Sunlight cracked the ash tree. Emma was in the beach chair, smiling, an odd, Leonardo smile. Lovely. How her face had deepened into itself. Years had italicized her expressions, registered at the corners of the mouth and eyes, and in the eyes. "You look enigmatic," I said. "Are you all right?"

"Yes. Let's hear about the trip."

I gave her a summary, ending with Jack's farewell but moderating it and my reaction to it. "It's such a relief to have the others more or less set. I feel like a camel that's come to the oasis after thirty-five years crossing the desert. He never wants to see sand again. Though there's Ben's kid. That'll be a little beach of it anyway."

Emma made a funny sound. I looked up. Mona Lisa seemed frightened. No, frightened plus something. Oh, God, I thought, she's got something. "What is it, sweetheart? Did Dr. Wanny find something? Don't worry. Tell me."

No, it was still a smile, just inflected a bit with puzzlement. She patted her stomach. Perhaps with Jack at the back of my mind I thought, oh, she's overeaten, she's got a bellyache. Or, it's her period. Then I realized what it meant. "Oh, no," I said. "Oh, Emma, no."

The blue eyes darkened, opened, and now did look afraid.

I went on. "You don't mean it. Not really."

"Yes. The Riemersphere is going to be enlarged."

The desert stretched ahead. I was fifty-five. Emma was patting what was longer than a ten-thousand-mile trip: twenty-odd years of fatherdom. Of rearing. Of bills. Of worry. Of every sort of emotional up and down. "I'm so sorry, Emma. I'm sure it's early. We can do something about it."

The brightness was all gone now. Her curls shook back and forth. "No, Cy. No. This is it. Mine. Ours. The one thing I'm going to finish. To have. With or without you. Full term. Graduation. Degree. All the way."

vi

New York. Two weeks after the second inaugural of the president who, on Emma's red heart, appears as "President Rin-Tin-Tin"—"He is our first professional-artist president, so I give him his due"—and "The Honorable Hibernian Hot-Air-Rises-to-the-Top, Mr. Holy Roller, the Great Ron." This last inscription silvered a good part of the red heart. It was adapted from Fitzgerald's *Crack-up*, the book sent to her in the hospital last year as an odd "delivery present," by none other than her eldest stepson. It was the first present Jack had given anyone in years. I should have guessed it was a sign of the turnabout, which had apparently begun—Jenny wrote me this—the very day of his Declaration of Nullity to me on Broadway.

Jack's second gift—a year later—was a plane ticket to New York. He'd offered tickets and hotel accommodations to every member of the family including Emma, our little George, and my grandchild, two-year-old Naomi.

I, however, am the only one who's come. Agnes is still in the Rwanda hills with the portable library—"Two hundred books in the back of a four-wheel-drive Roadmaster"— Jenny and Oliver are in Kuala Lumpur; Ben can't be derailed from *The Need to Hurt*. ("I wouldn't take off to see Mom hitched to the Pope, let alone to see Jack's dumbass program.") Nancy won't travel with Naomi "in this weather," nor will Emma with George. As for Livy, she's down with flu caught on her inauguration assignment. ("Looking for terrorists in Washington sewers.")

In the screening room at CBS, I sit with Jack and his producer, Vanessa van Siemens. I feel them eyeing me through the screening of this pilot. I try not to disappoint them. I laugh, groan, breathe heavily. Despite my delight that Jack has turned himself around in these last two years, I'm not particularly enchanted by his product. In fact, I'm dismayed by it. It's not the entertainment itself, which is like that of every other television series, a combination of Red Riding Hood and either Jack the Giant Killer or Jack the Ripper. Nor is it the milieu, a rich, decayed New York peopled by villains and pursuers with sophisticated armament and gnomic phrases. No, it is an important, supposedly minor character who absorbs me, the only *real* character in the show, the hero's father, Dr. Smithers, an Addled Intellectual whose misapprehension of the world triggers the trouble which his son, the detective, resolves. No, Dad Smithers is not the editor of a science newsletter, but a doctor whose highfalutin' carelessness makes trouble for his patients, his children, his poor wife, and his girl friends. "The father's the heart of the series," says Vanessa. "Every episode takes off from something he's done or some bad advice he's given. Jack hasn't decided whether the son will save the old guy or reluctantly send him to the slammer."

"Interesting concept," I say.

"Vanessa thinks it's going to be a winner, Dad."

"It's got a chance," says Vanessa.

"Not too bad, Dad, eh?"

"Wonderful."

Vanessa is pretty, smallish, thirtyish, blondish, soft-spoken, vaguely Texan. Jack says she has a history degree from Oxford. Clearly, though graciously, she calls the tune here. "The originality of Jack's script is that the hero's a new twist of the Hammett–Ross Macdonald hero, a free-wheeler, a dreamer, a really private private eye. Yet he isn't contemptuous of officials, doesn't think he's their superior. He believes in organizations and institutions. It's just that he doesn't like to rise and shine with the early birds. He doesn't want to catch the usual worm."

I'm tempted to tell her that the hero's creator spent much of his first fifteen adult years in the sack. I trim this to "Jack understands the type." I don't add that he doesn't under-stand the type's father.

The actor who plays that role doesn't look—small mercy—like me. He has a huge jaw and what I suppose are called sensuous lips. His philandering pains everybody and causes lots of trouble. He's a strong-looking man, that is, till his son reveals the selfishness, vanity, and resentment—of his son—which drive him.

"If you get any story ideas, Dr. Riemer, I hope you'll pass them on to Jack. You know how much he respects your judgment."

"I haven't had an idea since 1960." (I don't bother correcting her about this third honorary doctorate. There's obviously something in my manner which earns what I haven't.) "I know you and Jack will come up with everything you need."

"So far, so good. A lot of people think we have a winner here."

Vanessa can't have dinner with us. "I'm wooing a sponsor at Four Seasons, but it's been wonderful meeting you. You're the first member of a family I somehow know better than my own." She is slightly too deft to be charming, but, if only to overcome my unsteadiness at seeing Jack's version of me on the screen, I find all the virtues I can in her. I bend to kiss her good-bye, but her hand is at the end of her oustretched arm, so I shake it and wish her luck with the show. "This is the only one of the five shows I've been with that I can respect. I want to thank you for Jack."

"It's only Jack you thank for Jack. He's been all Jack a long long time. Any more of me in him, we wouldn't be here."

The night is clear and cold, lit with New York's electric jewels, the sort of night I've loved since boyhood when I'd walk downtown in a tuxedo pretending I was going to a cotillion at the Pierre. Jack is taking me to Lutèce. "I want to begin paying you back for all the meals you've bought me." In his cashmere coat and earmuffs, he looks odder than I've ever seen him.

Our table is under a skylight; a keel of gold moon sits in it. "Quite a place, Jack." There are no prices on the menu. "I have a feeling this meal will make up for all I've bought you. Not that I want you to make up."

A twenty-year-old Monbazaillac—which probably costs a hundred dollars—takes a few kinks out of me. Jack smiles paternally. I look sharply at him, and once again I see the boy I knew. "So what do you think, Dad?"

"I think you're fatter than a pig, Jack" is what I don't say. He has a settled-in heaviness that says, "This is what there is, take it or leave it." I say, "I think it's a success."

"Your kiss of death."

"Hell no. There's enormous skill there, even I can see that. All those violent, complicated problems proposed and settled in one hour. I don't see how you do it."

"It's more like half an hour. Thirty-eight minutes, actually. That's all we get on an hour show."

"I'm proud of you. You've mastered a skill thousands of people are failing to master. In two years, you've come from nothing to—this." I nod toward the white tables, the rich buzz and fuzz, the skylight with the little moonboat moored in it.

"You don't think it's contemptible stuff? What profiteth a man et cetera?"

"It's obviously of importance to people, or you wouldn't be able to afford this. As for profit, it's profit. Great corporations don't have souls to lose."

"I can't really afford it. Not yet. I'm showing off to you." This with the smile that, since childhood, showed his real sweetness. "I will soon though. In a couple of years I'll have more money than you."

In the same breath, he'd gone from sweetness to this. "I'm glad you'll have money. You may have to help me with your half-brother's tuition. As you'll probably have to sub for me at his graduation."

"Go on. George has revitalized you. You'll be a young seventy-six at his graduation. But I'll be there, maybe with my own kids then."

"Thank you, Jack. I wish you had them to see your triumph now. I wish Mom could be here. Maria too."

"I don't know about *that*."

"Are you in touch?"

"You might say that. She called a month ago to ask what I'd done with the silver. As if I'd pawned it."

I suppressed my suspicion. "I'm sorry."

"I'm not. It helps get her out of my head. Vanessa is ten times the woman she is."

"Oh? I didn't realize she was more than your producer."

"She's everything. Lifeline, consoler, protector, muse."

"That's fine, Jack. I liked her."

"But you didn't like the show."

"Yes, I did. I certainly was absorbed by it. And if it's the success your girl says it might be, I guess I'll be a sort of celebrity."

"I don't get that, Dad. Nobody gives a damn who writes these things. Why should they care about the writer's family?"

"I meant that your version of me will make me a sort of national villain."

"What in hell does that mean?"

"Aren't I the old sawbones? Smart-ass old troublesome Dad?"

Jack's eyes got as big as they ever got. Until now, I don't think he'd known. "Maybe. In a way. A very roundabout way."

"When Emma was in the hospital with George, you sent her that book of Fitzgerald's. I read it. Damn good. There was a paragraph in it about van Gogh's portrait of an old shoe. Remember it?"

"No."

"He says we have van Gogh's version of the shoe, but where's the shoe's version of van Gogh?"

"That's cute, but what does it have to do with the show? Or us? You haven't painted my portrait."

"I think you think I have. I've had this version of you, have thought about you in a certain way, have spoken to others about you that way, maybe even persuaded you that that's the way you are. I think you've resented it, and that this is your way of getting back at me."

"Quite a theory. You sure know how to throw words around, Dad."

"It's what I do, Jack. You're not too bad yourself."

"I'm not in your league. Which may be why I'm in television. Words don't count so much there. As for the father, you've got to admit he's the funniest character in the show."

"Funny? That I missed. Interesting, yes. And what the hell, where else should you draw characters from but people you know, people you feel strongly about? I just wish you didn't feel about me the way it shows up."

"I feel every way about you. But I don't want to hurt you. At least, I'm sure most of me doesn't."

"One way or another, it can't be helped. It's part of being father and son. I was wrong to mention it. I certainly don't want to stifle the biggest thing you've ever done by making you self-conscious about it."

"Too late for that. But it won't stop me."

"I don't think anything'll stop you now, Jack. Not even you yourself."

Back at the hotel, I kissed him good-bye. "Come see your little brother when you can."

"Maybe Christmas. I hope he isn't turning into another me."

"That would be all right with me," I lied. "I'll be more patient this time. Knowing how well it turns out."

The next day, flying back to Chicago, I did feel things

had turned out well enough. At least, I didn't have to worry about Jack. (Or only a little, and that mostly about his dramatic version of me.) My worry quota was filled by George and by the parental strikes against me: anxieties of age, money, and my capacity to handle anxiety itself.

I'd have to reconcile myself to shorter views. I might well not see George become whatever he'd become. That might make it easier for him. At least, he'd have lots of company, brothers, sisters, at least one niece.

I'd decided to put the *News-Letter* back in monthly gear. I needed the money. Emma edited copy and handled the business end of it. "With motherhood, it's the best job I ever had. And I do them in the same place." What was left of Grandpa Schein's money was being tucked away in IRAs for George's college. (There was going to be enough for Naomi's also.)

Sliding over the green lake toward the shore, I let myself yield to the bizarre, unearned excitement of coming home to a new family.

C.1

F   Stern, Richard G.,
STE   1928-

         A father's words